AND

HEARTLAND

Short stories from north-western Wales

Edited by
Dewi Roberts

Published with the financial support
of the Welsh Books Council.

ISBN: 0-86381-890-0

Cover design: Sian Parri
Cover illustration: Rob Piercy

First published in 2005 by
Gwasg Carreg Gwalch, 12 Iard yr Orsaf, Llanrwst
Wales LL26 0EH
℡ 01492 642031   🖷 01492 641502
🖑 books@carreg-gwalch.co.uk   website: www.carreg-gwalch.co.uk

Contents

Foreword

' . . . sun destroys/the interest of what's happening in the shade'
Philip Larkin famously wrote.

In an age of accelerating globalisation it sometimes seems
that regionalism in a small country like Wales is being shifted
further and further into the margins. That was one of the
incentives for compiling a selection of creative writing focusing
on a part of Wales which we have come to regard as the
heartland of the country. Although the term globalisation was
probably not in use when he wrote it, W.J. Gruffydd's story
Dripping Leaves has, to my mind, more relevance now, in a sense,
than when it was first published. A middle-aged man returns to
the square mile where he spent his youth. Here he reflects on the
people who 'lived in a small circle, seeing only small things,
thinking small thoughts and yet they had something in their
lives that he, for all his success and learning, did not have,
something he had not found in all his wanderings over five
continents'. Regions are clearly not geographical and cultural
parts of a country which, in an ideal world, should be consigned
to a peripheral position.

Each Welsh region is markedly disparate in so many ways
and Gwynedd and the Vale of Glamorgan are as opposed in a
topographical and cultural context as it would be possible to
envisage in a country the size of Wales. But, of course, it is these
very differences which make Wales as a whole such a
fascinating country and a land which continues to provide
stimulus for both fiction writers and poets.

In this selection north-western Wales is the setting for stories
by both Welsh language writers in translation and Welsh writers
in English. The region is evoked in varying degrees within the
stories. I use these words advisedly, for in some the locale is
made explicit, mainly through the use of place-names, whereas
in others the general ambience is suggested.

A number of the authors were born in either Gwynedd or on

Anglesey while the remainder first saw the light of day in Pembrokeshire, Carmarthenshire and Denbighshire. Chronologically the stories cover a comprehensive time span from W.J. Gruffydd and Kate Roberts, both born in the final two decades of the nineteenth century to Angharad Price, born in 1971.

The stories reveal some highly individual responses to relationships and experiences. We encounter a minister of religion who is prepared to be arrested on a matter of principle, a Liverpool woman who inherits a cottage in a Gwynedd village, a wife who is returning over treacherous waters to Bardsey in order to be with her sick husband, an adolescent boy who is heartbroken by the arrival of a letter. We read of a gay relationship in a story that is also set on Bardsey, while Robin Llewelyn's surreal contribution focuses on an erotic heterosexual relationship set on a small estuary island in Merioneth.

The compression of narrative, which the short story form demands, means that the skilled narrative of the genre is more difficult to achieve than is the case with the more loosely structured form of the novel. All the stories in this anthology illustrate this admirably.

Dewi Roberts

Introduction:

'The Square Mile'

It is a curious fact that technology has both shrunk our world, and enlarged it far beyond a graspable human scale in the same process. Fortunately for us the forces of reaction, in the form of literary expression, are on hand to mediate the resulting confusion. Crucially, we no longer live together as we would once have done. That marvellously acerbic scholar, poet and writer W.J. Gruffydd – who is represented in this collection by the elegiac story 'Dripping Leaves' – defined the point exactly, whilst at the same time celebrating what has been lost, in his volume of memoirs *Hen Atgofion: Blynyddoedd y Locust:*

' . . . my mind turns more and more to the old things and the old folk. The truth is that I have never lived in a community since I left Llanddeiniolen for Cardiff a quarter-century ago. Here I simply reside, sleep, work, eat – but I do not live here. At home in the village where I was reared [Bethel, in Arfon] I was part of one large community. I knew all about Elin Owen next door, and her husband Gruffydd Owen the sailor. When I heard laughter through the open window, I knew for certain who was there. And when a child passed me on the road, I could relate the histories of its father and mother and grandparents. I knew where its great-grandparents were buried, of what chapel they were members, and I could repeat for you many of their sayings. When I was a child, I could describe the mantelpiece of almost every house in the neighbourhood, knew in which of them were portraits on glass of Garibaldi, sets of *Y Gwyddoniadur,* a yellow cat called Sam or a glass rolling pin hanging on the wall. I knew how my neighbours would react in any situation, where I'd be received kindly, and where to keep silent about who I was.'

The short story in Welsh and Anglo-Welsh literature is the literary equivalent, the appropriate celebratory form, for that famous construct of D.J. Williams's, *'dyn ei filltir sgwâr'* ('a man of his own square mile'). It is pointless to look, in the short story as it is practised in the literatures of Wales, for the range of situation, locality and for the most part perhaps even resonance that we might find in Chekhov, de Maupassant or D.H. Lawrence. In its characteristic Welsh form (and it should be remembered here that short-story-writing scarcely existed in Welsh before the twentieth century), it is the literary expression of a society on the cusp, that found in this genre a graphic and economical means to give voice to its preoccupations. And how they cluster here: sexuality and its implications; the abiding presence of the past and its capacity to disturb; the changing nature and composition of a formerly local society. These are the recurrent themes, variously handled and approached, in the stories Dewi Roberts has assembled in his collection, all of them from a small geographical region of north-west Wales which is a crucial part of that beleaguered entity, *Y Fro Gymraeg*.

Their striking, shared characteristic is their commitment to evocation of sense of place. Even the supremely economical Kate Roberts, mistress of her craft and one of its supreme practitioners in world literature, devotes the first five paragraphs of the story with which the anthology opens to conjuring up the physical world in which it takes place. With every other writer here, the landscape peers insistently over his or her shoulder at the activities of the created human protagonists: Robin Llewelyn's lovers shimmer against the polished scales in the hide of little Ynys Gifftan; Brenda Chamberlain's *alter ego* shivers the night away alone on a boat in the tide-race, waiting for the whale-bulk of Ynys Enlli to slip like some Leviathan out of the mist and guide her back to her love and home; John Sam Jones's young men squirm through a narrow slit in the rocks to find physical release among the seals above the contained sway of the tide. Reality in all these tales is never more than a glance away, whether it be at the world around, of which we are being offered these glimpses, or back over our shoulders towards what has been, and will never be again. Or as W.J. Gruffydd expressed it in one of his most famous poems – counterpointing his story here:

'O holl gyflawnder bywyd,
Heno nid oes a ddaw
Ond cof am goed y Gelli'n
Diferu yn y glaw.'

('Of all life's fullness,/nothing will come to her tonight/but memory of Gelli's trees/dripping in the rain.')

And yet, in the hands of the accomplished writer, the dripping of that rain speaks across time to our essential humanity, and the local and personal become the transcendent; time and again.

Jim Perrin, Hiraethog, Ionawr 2005

A Summer Day

Kate Roberts
(Translated from the Welsh by Dafydd Jenkins)

We were sitting, we three girls, on a stone wall outside a farmhouse, drinking milk. I am not fond of milk, but I can drink it on a hot day after walking for a long time, not because it quenches thirst, but because it is one of the things that go with walking in the country on a hot day. To see it conveys something of the cool atmosphere of a dairy. And so it was with this milk; we became a little cooler as we drank, though its flat taste made us more thirsty. The farmhouse had a cool look; it was newly whitewashed, and there had been no rain to wash away the spots of whitewash which had fallen at the foot of the walls. The house looked quiet and calm as newly whitewashed houses do. The people of the house were sitting near the door with their hands folded; they had the quiet look of people overpowered by the first sudden heat of summer. The garden too showed signs of spring-cleaning; the potatoes newly banked up, and the dark fresh earth which had been below the surface showing now, with a strip of the old dry light-coloured earth to be seen here and there. There was neatness in the straight furrow and in the level beds of onions. The young gooseberries hung on the bushes like hundreds of little teats.

Refreshed after drinking the milk, we set off again on our

journey; from the porch the farmer's wife looked at us going, with her hand shading her eyes, and a look on her face that said: 'I'd rather you were walking than I.'

Outside the gate there was a stagnant pond; in it some ducks and a sow and piglets were enjoying themselves immensely. The sow was up to her belly in mud, and no swimmer in the sea ever looked happier. Some geese were feeding at the edge of the pond; they stretched out their necks after us. Then came a voice from somewhere behind the house, crying 'chick, chick, chick', and fowls without number and geese and ducks and pigs rose up and ran to answer the call like a crowd of townspeople running to a fight. We stood astonished at the power of words to move animals.

We went on along the cart-track over the shoulder of the hill. An occasional stream ran between white sandy banks across our path, and many times we knelt to drink the cold water from our hands. Then we washed our hands with the gravel, so as to make them feel soft.

We came to a clearing under the shadow of the trees, and lay down on the grass. To a casual glance, the world around us looked as though it were autumn; the young leaves of some of the trees were greenish yellow, and last year's dead bracken lay there, thick and brown. But a second look showed us the young bracken beginning to grow, grey-green in colour, with the tops of the shoots curling towards the ground. But it was no time for looking at things minutely, as we lay there on our backs like that. We saw everything with lazy eyes; so everything looked like one thing, and not like separate things. On the birch trees there were little leaves, grey on the under-side; but to us they looked like snow on the trees. The rim of the sky was far off, too far off for us to think of it for long without losing our senses; its colour was that blue you have so often wanted to have in a frock, but in vain. It was as though there were three rings of mountains about us, their black colour paling to a feeble grey on the horizon. We lay there literally warming ourselves in the sun.

We gave our bodies, which had been shrinking in knitted coats throughout the winter, to that god. Uncomplaining, we let his rays fall on our faces. From the distance came the unbroken sound of waterfalls, a far-off, soft sound. But not indeed an unbroken sound; for our hearing would deceive us again. The sound seemed to stop with a gasp, and then to go on as before. The sound sent us to sleep. The three of us awoke with a single thought – tea.

We went down to the village. There was no teashop there; but as we always did, we decided to knock at the door of some house and ask them to make tea for us. There were not many people at home, for it was a holiday. We saw an open door, and made for it as though that house had been our goal since we set out in the morning. A magnificent woman came to the door. A big rosy woman, with black eyes and hair. Her hair was tied in a knot on the top of her head. She must have been a beautiful woman when she was slighter. She was wearing high stays which drove her breast almost up to her chin. She had on a clean blouse with a high collar; the blouse was too small for her in every direction, and it made us feel hotter than we were. There was a certain cheerfulness about her and her house. She had a kind, open face and she granted our request.

'Yes, of course, in a minute, as soon as the kettle boils.'

We went into the house and sat down. Soon our eyes became accustomed to furniture instead of the trees and sky. The furniture was full of china, inside and out; there was hardly a square inch that had not some piece of china or other; and the surprising thing was that there was no dust there, and that everything was shining. There was a fire, with a lot of bright fire-irons around it. The fire had decayed into a pile of black lumps, with white dust along their edges, in the heat of the sun. Sitting beside the fire in an armchair was a young boy of about eighteen or twenty. It was some time before we saw him; for it took a little while for our eyes to get used to objects under the big chimney. My first feeling was surprise at seeing a young

14

man sleeping by the fire in a hot kitchen on a holiday. Then came curiosity, the curiosity of a person waiting for tea, and without anything better to do. What sort of boy was this? What sort of eyes had he, if he were to open them? Was he intelligent? What if he was to wake up, and to prove to be feeble-minded? How awkward it would be!

The woman was moving about busily, and there came to me the happiness that you feel in the sound of china when you want your tea badly. She put a clean cloth on the table, and smoothed the folds down with her hand; the cloth made a sound that was harsh to the ear. And at the same time there came from the woman a question that I never like hearing:

'And where do you come from, if I may make so bold as to ask?' Whenever I hear the question I tell myself I will tell a lie when I answer; and every time I am asked, I am caught so much without warning that the truth is out before I have time to think of a suitable lie.

'From B---' said I.

'Heavens!' said the woman, opening her eyes and showing unusual interest, 'that's the name that's been spoken oftenest in this house for a month now.' A shadow crossed her brow. 'Do you know Miss Jones from B--- who's a barmaid at the "Three Funnels"?'

'No, indeed.'

Without looking at the boy asleep in the chair, but giving her head a certain scornful shake in his direction, she said:

'*He's* got married to that barmaid at the "Three Funnels". He *has* done a pretty trick. He got the girl into trouble, and he married her three weeks ago; and he hasn't been near her since, and she hasn't been near him either. And he doesn't mean to go near her again ever, says he.'

I turned my head unconsciously towards the boy. I could not turn back, once I had begun to look at him. He was still sleeping. I noticed his mouth and jaw. They were very weak. It was a flabby, slack, wet, dribbling mouth. His face had an innocent look, but I thought to myself that a rake could look innocent in sleep. 'I wish he'd wake up,' I said to myself, 'so that I could see his eyes. Perhaps his face is strong when he's awake. The eye makes so much difference.'

His mother was going on:

'He was eighteen last November, and his pay's a pound a week. How he thought he was going to keep a barmaid on a pound I do not know. But he didn't mean to marry her. He didn't know her six months ago. But he began to go pub-crawling with people older than himself, and this is the result.'

She sighed.

'Why the boy couldn't see the value of a home I do not know. He's brought great sorrow on this house. We're respectable people, you know, and his father's an elder in the chapel. Since this business happened, his father and he haven't spoken a word to each other. And I have to live with the two of them and try to keep the peace.'

She looked at her son sadly, and with more tenderness she said:

'Here he is today, moving here from one chair to the other without washing himself or putting a collar on, instead of going to the ploughing match with the boys as he did a year ago. The wenches have come to something indeed, they don't think of anything but how to trap innocent lads.'

For the life of me I could not take my eyes off the boy. I wanted him to wake up, so that I could see what sort of boy he was. Was he as innocent as his mother wanted to make out? Perhaps he had a rake's eyes.

But what if he were to open his eyes and hear his mother talking to strangers about him? And I was the only one who understood his mother, for my two friends were English. To all intents and purposes, there were three deaf and dumb people in the room.

I do not know how long the mother would have gone on if I had stayed to listen. To me, the house was quite different from what it was when we went in. Then, it was a bright house full of china. It was a heavy house by now.

As I turned to the porch, I turned my head to look again at the boy and his flabby mouth. He was still sleeping on. I hoped he would wake up.

I thought for a moment he was going to wake up. No, he turned over on his side, sighed, and slept on. When we went out, we heard the sound of the waterfalls again. The pavement was white in the sunlight, and the burning stones dazzled us. I turned my head back again, and saw the mother looking after us with a dazed and dreamy look upon her face.

Dripping Leaves

by W.J. Gruffydd
(Translated by J. Walter Jones)

The dank April evening closed over the greenness of Little Lane, which rambled between the hedges of Hafodlas and the Goetre and rose gradually towards its end on the land of Penbryn. The middle-aged man who was walking along it could not have said that the rain had ceased. It had been coming down throughout the day, slowly and soundlessly, not so much in showers as in a kind of condensation from the misty air, and now in the dusk, when the drops could not be seen forming, it was hard for a man to judge whether it had turned to 'milking weather' or not. But the rain seemed of small account to this leisurely traveller: he stopped frequently, turning to look back on the windings of Little Lane, and to gaze through the mist over the hillocks on Hafodlas and Goetre, and to listen to the myriad whisperings of the fields that seemed more silent than silence itself. As he turned to continue his journey he gave an occasional sigh, not altogether of unhappiness, but rather of longing or that nostalgia of ours when we revisit what remains changeless while we are changing and growing old.

Not that he was old yet. In every bone and muscle and vein he felt the abundance of life: he was more alert, more sensitive, more deeply conscious of the voices of his surroundings than he had been, say, thirty years ago, when he could be called a young man. He knew that he could now drink even deeper of every fountain than when urged by the unquenchable thirst of youth. Now he had judgement, taste, balance; he had won the respect of others, and had come to know those qualities in himself that earned him his own respect. Yes, he had won respect, and that without having to be too respectable. Prosperity had come to him since he left his old parish, and he could now come to spend a holiday every year at his old home and know that his friends had no reason to feel ashamed of him. And enterprise had not yet gone out of his life; nor was it likely to for many a year.

He suddenly thought it strange he had not visited Little Lane for more than thirty years. Yet he knew every turn in it. Yes, every thorn-bush and bramble, every stone in the base of its hedgerows. This was the bottom of the Goetre Wood, where rabbits used to flock in June twilights: he could almost swear these were the same little white-tailed creatures as used to awaken the tenderness of Catrin in the old days. And here were the ferns both sides of the river – for river they called it hereabouts, though it was but a nameless and insignificant stream that flowed through the valley. Clear guide to the minds of the folk here, who had never seen anything big except the mountains of Snowdon to the south! What if they had seen the Danube at Vienna, or the Rhine, or even Severn or Wye? These were people who lived in a small circle, seeing only small things, thinking small thoughts – and yet they had something in their lives that he, for all his success and learning, did not have, something he had not found in all his wanderings over five continents. This very Little Lane of Penbryn – in the end, after more than a quarter of a century, he had been compelled to come back to it, to realise what he was, to find proportion when he looked back on his past.

It was hard to explain why he had so obstinately kept from visiting the spot that in his youth had been dearest of all to him. What inhibition through the years had forbidden him to come?

What vital urge had at last broken the ban?

By this time he had almost reached the middle of the Goetre Wood. No one ever came this way, even fewer now, no doubt, than thirty years ago. Here was the Erw Gron stile, almost overgrown by the long grass; it was difficult to make out any path leading from it across the field. Buses and cars were all the go now, and no one came this way. The rabbits had freedom to gambol at nightfall; even the peewits need have no anxiety about their nests on the floor of the bogland. No one came this way.

Neither did he see anyone in Little Lane thirty years ago, except old Humphrey the Foel, whom he sometimes met dragging himself feebly along to his evening rest after a heavy day's work on the Goetre land. 'Good night, gentlefolks,' was the old man's greeting whenever you met him; 'good night, gentlefolks,' to Catrin and me as we walked close together to the stile, 'good night.' And if it had been raining as it has today, he would add: 'Don't the trees drip to-night?' The Goetre Woods dripping, that was it, and the poor old Humphrey, weighed down by the burden of his years, wrapping the sacking more closely round his bowed shoulders.

My father used to tell me strange stories of old Humphrey's younger days. A bit of a rapscallion in his time, so they said.

There was that story of his courting the daughter of the Glyn. Humphrey at that time was a smart young fellow, to the fore in every local escapade. If there was fighting in the square at Tre'r Ceiri on Saturday night, you could be certain, my father used to reckon, that Humphrey was in the thick of it. If a new maid came to one of the farms, Humphrey would be the first to win her favour, and nobody else had a chance till he grew tired and cast about for a new conquest. Indeed, it wasn't one or two, but many at the same time, and he used to walk scores of miles every week, through all sorts of weather, to every corner of the parish a-courting. He would return in the early hours of the morning to snatch an hour's sleep before going to his work. Rapscallion, indeed!

But in the days when we – Catrin and I – used to meet him, no one would have believed these romantic stories. He was old then, bent, silent, done with every amusement in the whole wide world, done with courting and fighting, with all things gay and wild. Humphrey the Foel – a shadow in the dusk, in Goetre Wood, dragging his feet graveward. As the poet said of the garden-sweeper:

Another autumn – then will he
   Be with the leaves.

With the leaves. Those leaves that dripped in Goetre Wood only a spring ago.

In his prime Humphrey was the idol of the girls. His black eyes and curly hair, his shapely body and his merry laugh drove them all crazy. But of them all it was Lowri the Glyn who won his heart. She was the only one, my father used to say, who ever touched Humphrey's tricky affections or gave him pause in his progress from sweetheart to sweetheart. While he and Lowri kept company, his seat at the 'Horseshoe' was anyone's, and the daughters and maids of the neighbouring farms were left in comparative peace. Comparative, I say, for in Humphrey there was an urge that sent him wandering even when his heart was fastened on Lowri.

What came between them at last, I wonder? What burning words, what supplication, what refusal, what bitterness of weeping did the Glyn Woods hear? Marriage between Lowri and Humphrey was not to be thought of, for she was the daughter of a well-to-do farmer living on his own land, and had been to England for years of schooling. Humphrey was a farm-labourer, and besides, too irresponsible to make a satisfactory husband.

I wonder whether Father knew anything of this story? But it is too late to ask him now. Lowri went to London and married a worthy businessman, and the day after the quarrel Humphrey went to sea. Perhaps, had he been a little less hasty, he might have seen Lowri again. But he remained at sea or in some far-off place till that day when, after scores of years, he was seen back again, an old man, silent and harmless. Just as he was when he used to pass Catrin and me with his 'Good night, gentlefolks'. And Lowri was an old woman scheming to find matches for her daughters in the Philistine society of London. How unwilling she was to talk of the old place when occasionally I met her!

And here am I now, day-dreaming over the fate of Lowri the Glyn and Humphrey the Foel, both dust this many a year. As though my own youth, and Catrin's, had not been buried in the Goetre Wood! What can be said of this kind of fear: fear of the dead past, fear of the phantom of that awful day here under the trees of Goetre when I saw Catrin for the last time in my life? That rainy night. The eager meeting. The loving hands under the maple. And the quarrel almost from nothing: a spark that became a flame that was fanned into a roar. I know now that Catrin loved me as no one else ever loved me, and I know that I loved Catrin as I have never loved anyone since. What fools we were to part forever in anger and bitterness. With the drip-drip from leaf to leaf above our heads.

The dripping of the leaves, the dripping away of our lives!

A pang of that old longing stabbed the heart of the middle-aged man as he walked over the green ruts of Little Lane. For years he had trusted that the old wound was healed without a scar. This very night he had felt so sure of himself, so confident of his maturity and wisdom and that his life since had placed the woes of youth in perspective. Now, after closer self-examination, he could see that it was a kind of rashness, a challenge to the strength of his old grief, that had driven him thus to venture through the Little Lane of Penbryn. During long years he had deliberately closed his eyes and refused to acknowledge his own feelings; but in the depths of his soul there was fear – fear that the years would bring no healing.

Terror suddenly came upon him, and panic. Was the

memory of Catrin less keen to-night than that morning after the parting? What a fool I was to come here on a rainy night like this, with the drip-drip of the leaves in my ears!

He started running like a man who has seen a ghost. Then, suddenly, he slowed down. His heart was pounding, his feet refused to hurry, his shoulders bore the weight of the whole world. This would never do – never. A man so sure of himself to be giving way like this. He would go back to the house at once.

He had come nearly to the Penbryn cross-road. Between him and the grey light of dusk he saw coming in his direction a youth and a girl arm-in-arm, evidently lovers going for a walk through the Goetre Wood. The lane was narrow and he stepped towards the hedge to give them room. As they passed, the youth gave him a cheerful 'Good night'.

He gazed at them stupidly and answered in a low voice: 'Good night, gentlefolks – don't the trees drip to-night?'

The Wedding

John Gwilym Jones
(Translated from the Welsh by Islwyn Ffowc Elis)

'We are met together in the presence of God for the purpose of uniting these two persons . . . '

I am, like the marriage service, dignified enough, simple and unassuming enough, but painfully formal. Speaking it so often has made it as mechanical to me as my prayers and the burial service. I can easily say one thing with my voice while thinking of something quite different. In an unguarded moment I could speak of these persons here present putting on immortality. Many a time I have wondered what would happen if, instead of asking 'So-and-so, wilt thou have this man to be thy wedded husband?' I asked, 'So-and-so, wilt thou have so-and-so's heart?' and she sang. 'I will without dela-a-ay! My heart's belonged to Hywel for many a da-a-ay!' In these rash moments I feel like a giddy girl. But so things are, and so they will be.

And so I am, and so I shall be now. I am deep in the rut, and think of everything in terms of a preface and three heads. Soon I shall give advice to these two persons. I shall preface my remarks with the marriage at Cana of Galilee and the Lord Jesus's interest in the small joys of the children of men. I shall speak in the first place of the need to bear the one with the other in the wedded life; secondly, of the opportunities for

24

enrichment, the one in the other, in the wedded life; and thirdly and lastly of the propriety of giving pride of place to God, the Great Reality, in the wedded life. From now on I must, like the ploughshare, be content in the furrow. Only the crude, superficial experiences common to thousands will come my way. I hear the high wind and the heavy rain. I see the most prominent hilltops and the wide rivers. Gone is the morning of my life with its breezes and daisies. Come is the heavy afternoon with its dog daisies. I have formed a thick skin to take the insult here, the censure there. I have learned to count ten before answering back. I come and go between the bickering of elders and the death sighs of the faithful. I have lost all poise in trying to balance the factions. Like Pavlov's dogs I react instinctively, unconsciously, to specific sounds at specific moments. 'Earth to earth, ashes to ashes,' says my voice, and my face unknown to me forms the tearful expression expected of it. 'I baptize thee, Peris Wyn,' says my voice, and my face involuntarily melts into a smile. 'This is my body, This is my blood,' says my voice, and I am clothed from head to foot in the essential, traditional gravity.

Yet, when John Llywelyn's letter came . . . 'It is you who christened us both and received us both into membership, and we would like you to marry us . . . ' I could not help being proud. I felt that my life had not been entirely in vain. Weaned from the ambitions of youth, from its visions and hopes and joys, I grew into the tepid, monotonous ordinariness of a good minister of Jesus Christ and contented myself with my lot. This is my cross, but under its weight I have felt as much earthly happiness as is possible and fair to the likes of me. I have been faithful over a few things, and I know I shall enter fully some day into the joy of my Lord.

'Who presents this woman to be married?'

'I present her.' And good riddance to her. I step forward, squaring my shoulders lest that wife of mine or my brother Wil or any of the family whose company we requested the pleasure of here think that I care a damn for any of them. Tonight I shall go to Davy John's shop and I shall say, 'Two ounces of shag, Davy John.' 'Two ounces?' he'll say, stressing the word 'two' like a reciter. 'Yes, two,' I shall say, my stress as good as his, throwing down my money like a lord at the races. And the next week I'll buy three ounces. The butter and the tea and the sugar will last longer with one mouth less to feed. The week after I'll get myself a new pair of boots. Come the end of the month I'll go to town to G.G.'s to be measured for a suit with a stripe in it. 'What d'you think of this one?' I'll say, off-hand like, to my brother Wil. In less than a year I'll be offering my tobacco tin to Jones, the quarry steward. 'Have a pipeful, Mr Jones?' 'I don't smoke shag.' 'Neither do I . . . . '

'Catrin, where's my stud?' 'How should I know? Where did you put it?' 'If Lizzie Mary were here she wouldn't take long to find her father's stud . . . ' 'This rice pudding isn't as good as usual.' 'Isn't it?' 'Too watery by far.' 'I haven't made any for years. Lizzie Mary always made it . . . ' 'Catrin, did you bring Y *Faner*?' 'Drat, I forgot.' 'Lizzie Mary never forgot her father's paper on a Wednesday night . . . ' Well, as Twm-Yes-and-No always says in the Literary Society, there's so much to be said for one side and the other that I can't decide. I think I'll abstain from voting.

'*John Llywelyn Evans, wilt thou have this woman to be thy wedded wife?*'

'I will.' The organ pipes are neatly arranged according to size, those at both ends looking so tall and thick because those in the centre are so small. It is a comparative matter. And somewhere in the middle there are two, of which I cannot tell with certainty which is the taller. I know that if Mr Lewis struck the sounds that emerge from them there would be at least half a tone between them, and then my ear would catch the difference.

I should like to be a critic able to list the books of the ages in order of merit. That, of course, is impossible. It would not be difficult to choose the books at both ends. My large pipes would be the Bible and the *Mabinogi*. 'Yes,' my critics would say, 'we agree that the Bible should be at one end, but why the *Mabinogi*? Have you never heard of Euripides and Tacitus and Shakespeare and Cervantes and Dante and Balzac and Tolstoy and Goethe and . . . ?' 'Yes of course, I have heard of them all, but I am a Welshman.' 'Ah,' they say, like schoolmasters, 'but literature is above nationality. You must not think within the confines of your own land; you must reach out, spread your wings, and see an author and book in their proper place in the growth of the literature of the whole wide world; you must acquire a classical mind and learn to compare and contrast and see how much one author learned from those who went before him. And then decide whether he added to the riches or merely lived off the riches of his forebears. A good critic must know whence came a lyric and a novel. They are not things made of nothing, hovering in air, unconnected as gossamer. That is sheer romanticism, criticism that is nothing but personal taste, a whim.'

I know that all their arguing has a cruel logic. But for me there is no argument wrought in the minds of men that can topple the *Mabinogi* from its pedestal. Myfanwy and Ceridwen and Eluned have more beautiful names than Lizzie Mary. Miss Davies at the County School probably knows more about cookery than Lizzie Mary. Jane Tŷ Gwyn has a sweeter temper and Megan Tŷ Capel lives nearer the mark. Lizzie Mary's mind is made of English penny dreadfuls and newspaper headlines and Hollywood movies: I'll admit it. She has very little idea of politics or literature, and Reaction and Revolt in the one as in the other mean nothing to her. But she's my sweetheart, and that's all that matters. Will I take this woman to be my wedded wife? I wi-i-ill without dela-a-ay! My hea-a-art's belonged to Lizzie for many a da-a-ay! You'd be frightened out of your wits if I sang like that, wouldn't you, the Reverend Edward Jones? You'd be surprised at how near I am to doing it. There's Lizzie Mary handing her bouquet to her sister Gwen, and Robin fumbling with finger and thumb in his waistcoat pocket for the ring. He is very fond of the Mabinogi too. Poor Robin!

'Lizzie Mary Jones, wilt thou have this man to be thy wedded husband?'

'I will.' There: I have spoken the words simply, coolly, feeling nothing more than the reasonable excitement of any bride. This is not how I imagined my wedding. There was a time when I saw myself as the young man's fancy. I wandered with him through the white wheat and sauntered along the paths of the sheep till we reached the green blade of grass. But at last, after many tribulations, after bearing the cruelty of father and mother, after writing with blood from my own arm, I was forced to stand beside Maddocks in church, wretched as a faded lily. Behind me sat my proud family; beside me, haughtily, Maddocks was marrying my body while outside, somewhere, breaking his heart, was Wil. Don't break your heart, Wil. Soon the Maid of Cefn Ydfa will lie still in her grave and Wales will be singing your idyll . . .

There was a time when I imagined myself saying 'I will', trembling with a comsuming passion. Beside me stood a powerful he-man, a man among men, not unlike Clarke Gable in *I Adored Her*. He had one of those haggard attractive faces with wavy, brilliantined hair and a cheeky little twist to the corner of his mouth. I felt exhilarated at having humiliated him and bewitched him into saying 'I will' with such humble gratitude; yet the touch of his hand on mine as he placed the ring made me flesh, every inch of me. I stood there brazen, abstractions like morality and chastity and temperance having ceased to be, even quite tangible things like my father's frown and my mother's smack and the tongue of Betsan Jones next door having become as nothing in the world to me . . .

Another time I would marry above my station. Behind me would sit my mother. 'A Triplex grate, wooden bedsteads, a three-piece suite and a carpet,' she would say to herself. 'I'm taking a fortnight's holiday this year,' my father would say to the quarry steward, 'to stay with my daughter at Bumford Hall.' 'I'm off to Paris,' my sister Gwen would say. 'To Paris?' 'Yes, with Lady Elizabeth.' 'Lady Elizabeth?' 'My sister, Lady Elizabeth Bumford, you know . . . ' But here's what happens. I am marrying one of my own kind, not forced and not feeling anything other than the ordinary thrill of any girl on her wedding day. I say 'I will' quite simply, seemingly unconcerned, perfectly satisfied and perfectly happy because I know I am doing the right and the wise thing to do.

'Then let the man place the ring on the fourth finger of the woman's left hand.'

There's the ring on her finger. Now I am a man who covets his neighbour's wife, a fornicator in my mind, a victim of unease and the weariness of things half done, a soul without a body. For me there will be bouts of lust without the forgiveness that follows lusting with another, and afterwards the drowsy torpor in loneliness. And pain and guilt the next morning, because I can never free myself from the chains of the Ten Commandments or the bonds of the thousand and one commandments of my home. Thou shalt not commit adultery, thou shalt not bring false evidence, thou shalt not play cards on Sunday, thou shalt not put a shilling on a horse, thou shalt not imbibe strong drink. I do all these things, gnawed by the traditional guilt of a child of the *seiat*. I am robbed of the delight of sin and of the short-sightedness that sees only the single isolated act.

Last night I tossed and turned for hours. Tonight it will be worse. To tame myself I stretch and tauten every muscle. I wind myself into a ball, my arms tight around my legs, my chin on my knees. I beat the pillows with the monotonous rhythm of a piston. I tire of this and turn, suddenly furious. I turn again. Again and again I turn. And all this time the thing will be working its way through my mind, creeping and wallowing there like a frog in slime . . . But at this moment I am perfectly happy; indeed, better than happy. I can observe myself last night and tonight and every night without emotion, without prejudice, and see the abomination, not because the Old Testament and my mother have taught me so, but because I have experienced a mystical uplift, a purification. My mind has been cleansed, and in this brief cleanliness I can observe myself last night and tonight as a stranger. I am more critical, I see more clearly the futility and the waste of energy. But they are the futility and the waste of energy of another man – not mine. Bred within me is the integrity of a good critic, who sees faults without prejudice and notes them without malice. They are not my faults, therefore I am not obliged to make resolutions. It is not for me to smother the lust of another man who lived last night and will live again tonight.

I wonder if it is by giving us this glimpse of the old man and making us feel the strangeness of him that Jesus Christ forgives our sins? This joy is well known to me. Always, it is something from without that forces it upon me: poetry, a good sermon, a Bach fugue, a clear argument, pictures, acting, a high mass I heard once.

And today, the marriage covenant in accordance with the holy ordinance of God. By my side, John Llywelyn shivering as he used to do after a cold dip in Llyn Hafod Ifan, when we are all pain without but warm with joy and life within. Gwen, the sounds of the service giving her drowsy eyes the happy look of the young when they contemplate their end. I can imagine her composing a sonnet: 'When my frail corpse is lowered to the grave . . . ' Old Edward Jones with his honest intonation turning this ring, and I do solemnly declare, and so that you may stand before God when the secrets of all hearts are revealed, into pure worship. In the fine breeze of this sanctification I can look at Lizzie Mary without coveting her, and feel her closeness without lewd thoughts. This is the purification, the beauty absolute. It gives me forgivingness (don't ever mention those ten pounds again, Evan Hughes), and jocularity (you fell, did you, Huw *bach*, come here, let me pick you up), and humility (I am not worthy), and a bit of boasting too (I can do all things).

'Inasmuch as John Llywelyn Evans and Lizzie Mary Jones have made a convenant together in marriage . . . '

Today I am seventeen. I stand in the big pew in Penuel dressed in blue silk beside Lizzie Mary, my sister, who looks surprisingly self-possessed in white. I am very, very happy. Yesterday I was in school listening to Miss Rees's usual drivel. Her questions are as inevitable as the sore on her lip. That sore is her souvenir of the Great War. It was in that war that she lost her sweetheart. Which mutation follows *yn*? Why is *eu gilydd* incorrect? What is an anchoress? Where is Sarras? Who was Moradrins? Spinsterish, barren trivialities like herself. But I won't think about her and her type. I shall think about the adventurous things and the beautiful things in my life, such as learning for the first time the difference between the male and the female of the white campion; the breeze that cools the scent of the gorse; wetting my feet in Cae Doctor river and having my feet wet all day without catching cold; finding the nest of a hen that lays out; being ill and having neighbours bring me calves' foot jelly; closing my eyes and wondering who will cry for me when I'm dead. Lizzie Mary's wedding day will be among them. Some day little Gwenhwyfar will sit on my lap and ask, 'Mam, what were the nicest things that happened to you?' And I shall say, 'Well . . . finding a double-yolk egg . . . and your Aunt Lizzie Mary's wedding day . . . and . . . '

But what did I say? Little Gwenhwyfar? Mam? Today Lizzie Mary is consecrating herself to be a mother. In our family tree her name will be coupled with John Llywelyn's. I wouldn't like to be like Queen Anne alone in her family tree. Although she too probably had a sore on her lip . . . I am the Holy Grail. I am the sacred vessel preserved by Joseph of Arimathea. Here I stand, in the court of Pelleas, grandfather of Galahad, in all the glory of my holiness, pure, intact, like the Virgin Mary, incorruptible, immaculate. Who comes now on a pilgrimage from Arthur's court in Camelot? Who is this with the golden spur on his right foot? Burt? Lionel? Percival? Galahad? Come, my Galahad! Come, predestined seeker of the Holy Cup. Delay with hermits along the untrodden paths of dark forests, but come! Tarry awhile with sweet maidens in wooded vales, but come! Deliver monks from the excommunicate bodies in their sacred burial grounds, but come! Slay your ten knights and slay your forty, but come! Be sad at the burial of Percival's sister, but come! Come, and I shall nourish thee with my spiritual food, I shall show thee my secrets, I shall anoint thee king of my realm. Come! Come!

'And now the Reverend Arthur Davies will read a portion of the Scriptures.'

'The Lord is my shepherd, I shall not want . . . ' This is my first church, and my first wedding since I was inducted here, but I was not asked to officiate. I realize, of course, that memories and affection bind John Llywelyn and Lizzie Mary to their old minister, but for the life of me I cannot help being offended. These things always happen to me. I have always come second. To mother, I come second because my brother Robin smiles more readily and sees more quickly his chance to do a good turn. I was always second in my class at County School simply because Bobi Tan y Wern had more ability. It was second class honours, second section, that I got at College, and it was only after Rolant had turned down this church that it was offered to me. No one is ever unjust to me. That's the trouble. If there were injustice it would all be so much easier to bear. Always there are ample and adequate reasons why I should be set aside, and I can see them and admit the fairness of them. Something always stands between men and fulfilment. I begin everything I do knowing full well that my success will be only middling, and therefore I cannot throw myself body and soul into anything. One part of me does what it ought to do, while the other just wanders.

I want to consecrate myself wholeheartedly to my work . . . to penetrate into the mystical awareness like Saint John of the

Cross and Saint Teresa and Ann Griffiths. Gwen Jones is a pretty little piece. Really to know the love which casteth out fear. I wonder how old she is. That my soul might die unto itself to live in God. She's not too young. To walk in the light that makes the miraculous birth and the resurrection as natural as the drawing of breath. There's passion in those sultry eyes. To swoon in the heavenly bliss. Those full lips and young breasts. Green pastures. Under a hedge . . . Oh Lord, why must I be plagued with this eternal duality? Why must I be this hybrid of holiness and lust? Why can't I be either all body or all soul? Why cannot my passions run loose, free of the preventive power of Thy breath of life? Why cannot my soul leap and dance free of the fetters of lust? Why can't I be a body-soul and soul-body, inseparable as a compound word? The one to make mild the other, the other to enliven the one? So that in following Thee I shall possess Gwen and in desiring Gwen be in love with Thee? Such a thing is possible. I will make it possible . . . but who am I to will anything? I too shall set out, like Percival, on my adventure. I shall wander through the woods where birds sing. I shall fight with the serpent and see the ship of white samite. I shall speak with the man who bears the name of Jesus Christ on his crown, and lose blood from a wound in my thigh. I shall arrive at the court of Pelleas and my eyes shall behold the glory of the Sacred Cup. But it is Galahad who will see his adventure completed; Galahad, the predestined seeker, who will find his Holy Grail.

'And now may the grace of the Lord Jesus Christ and the love of God and the fellowship of the Holy Ghost be with you now and evermore. Amen.'

Relatives

Alun T. Lewis
(Translated by Hywel Teifi Edwards)

My uncle Edward was a bank manager in Deganwy, that historical spot where the river Conwy seems to hurry before thrusting into the sea and subsiding. We called him Uncle Ted and his wife Aunty Bet. She was my mother's sister. She always addressed him as Edward and in conversation with his wife I never heard him use any name other than Elizabeth. That's the kind of couple they were, rather fastidious, proper and very courteous; it was just that such unrelenting good manners inhibited a creature as unruly as a ten-year-old country bumpkin. It took so little to excite my aunt and when agitated she would move the china dogs and the brass candlesticks on the mantelpiece, or the dishes on the dresser, back and forth, needlessly, all the while breathing in and out quickly through her nose like a sexually aroused hedgehog.

But they were very kind and we would spend a fortnight or more every August in the fifth house from the end after crossing the railway bridge, where the row of houses forms an arch directly above the river's bed.

The river flowed deep and swift on its course and the stony beach sloped steeply from the narrow promenade. Across the river on Conwy's sea marsh were flats and sand dunes as there were nearer the sea towards Llandudno beach where the river now widened and coasted along.

But in this trough, opposite Glanaber, hardly anything was ever still – although aunty expected me to be – except for a short while when the tide turned. At that time, you could see a cluster of seaweed, or a twig or a ball swirling on its spot; but very quickly the tide would ebb, sweeping swiftly towards the sea between Anglesey and Great Orme's Head. Then, in its own good time, it would race back just as swiftly and the little boats riding at anchor would turn their noses, pointing at the estuary to sniff the breeze blowing over Conwy and Llansantffraid from the uplands of Hiraethog and Aled, passing Bryn-y-Maen church as it came.

Tom Huws fled from Port Dinorwic because, as the poet put it, nothing changed there but sun, wind and rain. Deganwy's splendour for me lay in the fact that everything happened there – in due course.

It was through watching the boatmen there that I learnt that the target isn't always reached by the direct route. With the run of the tide, when the river's course would be brim-full from bank to bank, they would have to row energetically against the current, halfway to Conwy and then turn the boat's prow and slip quickly, a little aslant, on the tide before landing directly opposite the starting-point.

I no sooner hear the doleful mewing of the seagulls as they follow the plough in the very early spring than I am transported for a moment to that little loft above the door in Glanaber, where I have got up in my nightgown to listen to the seagull on the roof and to look through the window to see the boats, all of one mind, tugging at their ropes – sometimes towards the sea and sometimes towards Conwy's bridges. I wasn't enough of a scientist, neither did I have the patience, to watch closely and see the turn of the tide.

We went occasionally past the golf-course to the sandy beach where I would be allowed to build sand-castles and dig ditches and paddle – 'You're surely not going to let him go to the beach in those clothes?' said aunty. 'What if you should see someone that we know!'

But the ideal place to play was the jetty. It was a wooden gangway, with handrails on each side, resting on hardwood piles cut and shaped for their purpose. The actual landing-stage, of the same black, hard wood, was at the far end of the jetty; it lay top-heavy and limp on the stones when the tide was low and rose gradually as it came in, the handrails levelling out, the gangway less steep and easier to traverse to the landing-stage, which came to life and heaved up and down sensuously as the tide fondled and jiggled it.

The big event of each day – except Sunday – was the arrival of the steamer from Conwy to pick up passengers from Deganwy and Llandudno and carry them up the river to Trefriw. But not always to Trefriw, mind, only when the tide was high enough; failing that you had to make do with Tal-y-Cafn. They were small, jaunty ships each with a straight-backed funnel belching smoke and two big paddle-wheels on each side like huge mill-wheels, churning the water into a great froth.

We didn't venture on board one of them for some years despite many a prod and a hint from me. Sometimes, I surmised that my father was too poor to afford the trip, but thanks to that strange instinct present in both animals and children, I half comprehended that Aunt Bet was the stumbling-block. I didn't think she was afraid of drowning, she came with us once on a steamer from Llandudno round Anglesey. A wind blew up that time before we reached Holyhead and she was seasick. I'll always remember that man telling her, 'Turn your head the other way missus!' But there was little danger of that happening either on the still waters of the Conwy! It remained a mystery to me until the hot summer of 1911 when my father, with my enthusiastic backing, persuaded her to go on the trip to Trefriw.

* * *

My aunt was very reluctant. 'That old man will be on the ship,' she said.

'Nonsense!' said father. 'Joshua Gruffydd is alright in his place.'

'Yes,' answered Aunty Bet in a steely voice, 'the trouble is that he doesn't know his place. And I have Edward's position to think about.'

But, as I said, she came. I was in my Sunday best, 'like a little gentleman', to quote my aunt, but prancing in a most ungentlemanly way on the beach seeing the ship pass the landing-stage, turn noisily, and pull in, the sailors yelling and two of them jumping on to the jetty to wind ropes around the bollards.

Then the gate at the far end of the jetty was opened and we went on board.

'We'll go ahead to keep us a place, Hannah,' said my father to my mother, and he said to me, 'You come along with Aunty Bet.'

My uncle, of course, was at the bank.

My aunt grasped me firmly by the hand in case I should fall in the river and I was glad that the Llangarrog boys weren't there to see me being treated like a baby just beginning to crawl.

Within two minutes we were ascending the gangway to the ship's deck, me eyeing everything eagerly, the great wheels, the bridge where the captain stood in all his glory, and under the bridge a hole leading to the depths of the ship.

As we were passing to go in search of my father and mother a sailor came up from somewhere below and stood in the hole like a picture in a frame. He wore a blue jersey and baggy trousers with a belt around his middle. His cheeks and chin were blue-black, not because he was growing a beard but because he hadn't shaved for two or three days.

Aunty Bet saw him and began to sniff and look agitated. She took hold of my hand clumsily, grasped it tightly and began to drag me after her, and the man said, 'Well blow me down! Betsy!'

My aunt stood transfixed as if confronted by a wall.

Then she turned and faced the sailor.

'How are you, Joshua Gruffydd?' she said dryly.

'I'm surviving, Betsy *fach*,' he said, 'just to avoid funeral costs. I've no money in the bank, you see.'

He extended his hand, black with coal dust, especially under the fingernails, but aunty ignored it.

'You have enough time to loaf around like this?'

The sailor smiled, showing two uneven rows of yellow teeth. 'He who made time, has made plenty of it, you see, Betsy.'

He looked at me. 'Good God,' he said, 'whose boy is this? That little man has never – '

I felt a sudden tug at my hand which made me feel that my arm was being disconnected.

'Come, Dewi,' said my aunt, 'your father and mother will be wondering where we've got to.'

And away we went, Aunty Bet with her nose in the air dragged me after her, my feet stuttering along in pursuit of my head as I turned back for another look at the strange man who had upset my aunt so much.

'Don't drag your feet,' she said, in a fiercer tone than I had ever heard her use before. 'Don't mind that old man, and don't you dare tell anyone about this ever.'

In a trice we had got to the ship's stern and had found my mother and father.

'I knew that we shouldn't have come,' snuffled my aunt. 'The day has been spoilt for me. That common old man.'

'Oh! You saw Joshua Gruffydd,' said my father. 'Don't let that spoil this glorious afternoon. Sit back and enjoy this incomparable scene.'

And it was beautiful, the water so calm and we now ready to land on the quay in Conwy.

'Look,' said mother, 'there's the smallest house in the world, and there's the castle, and there's Telford's bridge with the railway bridge behind it.'

'How will we go under the bridge?' I asked.

'Questions, questions,' said mother.

'They lower the stacks on their side,' said my father. The ship reversed a short distance from the quay and then started again towards the bridges.

I was determined to see the ceremony of lowering the stack, and I told my father that I was going to find a spot amidships where I could see everything clearly.

'Go with him, Huw David,' said my Aunt Bet. 'What if he should fall overboard?'

'Tut,' said my father, 'let him go. You mollycoddle him too much, Elizabeth. The boy must learn to stand on his own feet.'

And away I went, hardly hearing my mother say, 'Take care.'

By the time I got amidships, the bottom of the stack had been released on one side and two sailors were ready on the other side to pull on a rope to turn it on its side, and lower it, while the captain stood on the bridge awaiting the exact moment to give the command.

'Lower the stack.'

And they pulled on the rope so that the stack folded like that picture of the tower of Pisa I once saw in a book in school, and we sailed gracefully with the tide, under Telford's steel ropes and the steel box of the railway bridge, as if the little ship genuflected humbly and thankfully in recognition of the right to pass under on its way to the splendours of the Vale of Conwy.

Then, another shout from the bridge, 'Raise the stack', saw them pull on another rope, and the stack stood erect after its salaam to the keepers of the vale. The ceremony was over.

All around me were sitting down again but I decided to go forward, retracing my steps past the hole that opened on the mysteries of the engines.

Would that man be there, I wondered.

Tremors of expectation ran through me. I knew that my aunt Bet wouldn't approve of this, although I didn't know why.

I wanted to see the sailor again, and yet I was also afraid of seeing him.

The sun warmed the nape of my neck and I paused awhile, leaning over the deck-rails to watch the ship's bows cleaving the water. When I got near the bridge I was in the shade, and after reaching the opening to the ship's maw, I ventured to put my head inside, and felt the hot air playing around me.

And who should be there, just about to descend some iron steps, but the man I had seen before, the man who had been so forward with Aunty Bet.

I suppose I shut out the light and he turned his head.

'Hello,' he said. 'No one is allowed down here.' He came a step or two nearer. 'Oh,' he said, 'it's you again.'

'Tell me,' he said, bending down and looking me straight in the eye, 'is that woman you were with related to you?'

What a daft question!

'Of course she is,' I said, 'she's Aunty Bet. She has to be related to me then.'

'Huh! You are clever. Whose boy are you? And don't say your mother's boy. I know that much about this old world. What's your mother's name?'

'Mrs Oliver,' I said. 'She's the wife of the Revd David Oliver, Llangarrog.'

The sailor took hold of my shoulder, gripping me like a blacksmith's tongs. 'Your mother,' he said, 'what's her name?'

I was sorry I had gone there and I turned my head to see if my father or mother or Aunty Bet were anywhere in sight, but they were not.

'Hannah,' I said.

The fingers of the tongs that seemed to want to come together in the flesh of my shoulder relaxed their grip and the rough voice softened.

'Well! Well!' he said. 'Hannah's boy is it. I'm a half-brother to your mother, you see.' Then a second or two later. 'And to her sister, Betsy,' he said, in an angry tone again.

I didn't know what a half-brother was, but I was less afraid.

'What's your name?'

'Dewi.'

'Dewi. Well, Dewi, don't you want to know what my name is? And I your half-uncle.'

I was beginning to pluck up courage by now. 'What is your name, uncle?' I asked.

'Aha! That's better. Uncle is it! My name is Joshua. Have you heard about him? He was the man who made the sun stand still. But you shall call me Josh – because we're related – Uncle Josh.'

'Thank you, Uncle Josh,' I said.

My new uncle chewed tobacco all the time, and a yellow dribble ran from the corner of his mouth, along his chin and meandered through the stubble of his beard.

'Would you like to come down to see the boilers and the engine?'

That's what you would call being a man! I knew enough English to understand the significance of the words 'No Admittance' above the door. And I was being admitted!

The steps were full of drainage holes and made of cast iron and the heat increased as I descended, step after step, behind Uncle Josh. After reaching the bottom, we walked along an iron landing again, with rails on each side, and two pistons of gleaming steel thrusting back and forth regularly were attached to the cogs of the two big wheels which churned the water outside driving the ship onward.

The engine-room was at the far end of the path; a huge stack of coal half filled it and there was a hole in the roof through which the coal was delivered.

It was insufferably hot there. I removed my jerkin.

'Yes, take your coat off,' said my uncle, 'and I'll take off my jersey. I'll have to stoke a bit of these boilers. You sit on that box there.'

I obeyed and sat on a wooden box which had been turned upside down in the middle of the room.

My uncle took hold of a huge long iron hook and clawed open the door of one of the two furnaces, the heat striking me in my forehead and the sudden burst of light from the white-hot fire blinding me for a minute. Then my uncle spat on his palms, grasped the shovel and threw shovelful after shovelful into the heart of the fire.

What a muscular man he was! Sweat poured down his face, his vest stuck to him like a wet rag and the tufts of black hair in his armpits glistened in the firelight as he turned to lift another shovelful.

He finished shortly, shutting the furnace doors with a clang, but I had started sweating by this time.

Uncle Josh came and sat beside me on the box, the smell of sweat filling my nostrils. I also noticed a black smudge of oil on the sleeve of my white shirt.

My uncle saw me staring at it. 'Tut,' he said, 'a little dirt never harmed anyone.'

If only every adult was that sensible!

'My Aunt Bet will scold me,' I said disconsolately.

'Oh! Betsy is it! Not your father or mother. Are you afraid of her then?'

'Yes, I am,' I said, angry with him for forcing me to admit it, 'but her name isn't Betsy. My father and mother call her Beth, and Uncle Ted calls her Elizabeth.'

'Huh! That little penny-counting doll! Other people's money at that! The snob! At home in Y Lleiniau she was called Betsy, and your mother was little Hannah. She was the last little arse in the nest, you see.'

I didn't know what that meant, either. That was another question I would have to ask my father. I could ask him. But I wasn't going to show Uncle Josh my ignorance.

'Another five minutes before you go back on deck,' he said, taking a box from his trouser pocket and a two-bladed knife. From the box he took a roll of black tobacco, not unlike liquorice except that it was thicker, and harder, too, I guessed, judging by the way he had to use the knife to cut a piece. He spat once more and the yellow juice sizzled on the side of the furnace. He put a fresh quid in his mouth and started chewing anew.

'Is it nice?' I asked.

'Nice! Yes of course! But not sweet, mind you, sweet like London mouse shit. This is lovely and bitter and warms your insides.'

'What's London mouse shit?' I said, hurrying over that word so as not to hear myself saying it.

'Those small, small sweets of all colours. We used to buy a fistful of them for a ha'penny in Siân Price's shop a long time ago.'

'Hundreds and thousands,' I said.

'Good Lord! A scholar too! A fluent Englishman! I wonder what Betsy calls them by now?'

'Aunty Bet says "Pw",' I said, my mind still on that prohibited word.

'Pw!' My uncle laughed so much his belly wobbled. 'That's baby talk you see, Dewi,' he said.

Calling me a baby and I nine years of age and already able to swim!

'Aunty Bet says you are common,' I said, like some David picking up a smooth pebble from the river.

My uncle sobered instantly and his face changed.

His eyes narrowed like pigs' eyes.

He stared at me, almost sullenly, his forehead furrowed.

'Does she!' he snorted. 'The old bitch.'

Then he changed again just as quickly and smiled broadly; but the eyes narrowed even more.

'Never mind, Dewi, my lad,' he said. 'Hi, would you like to try this baccy?'

I didn't dare refuse. 'Yes I would,' I said.

He cut a piece with his knife and gave it to me.

'You have to chew it mind, not swallow it. You'll have to learn to spit then. Is there a spittoon in Betsy's house?'

44

'Yes, a brass one, in the fireplace; and my aunt polishes it every week. Is that what it's for?'

'Yes of course. You spit in that. You'll be a proper sailor then. AB Dewi Oliver, by damn!'

'What's an AB?' I asked. I was asking more questions than any sailor or man should . . .

'Able-bodied seaman,' said my uncle.

I put the quid hesitatingly in my mouth. Its taste was worse than the wormwood mother used to give me when I was constipated, or when she wanted to prevent me having tapeworms. In a minute or two my mouth was full of the bitter juice, and I was afraid to swallow after my uncle's warning.

And afraid to spit, too!

I had to swallow some of it, and then I started to choke and beads of seat stood out on my forehead. My uncle was somewhat startled and he leapt to his feet slapping the palm of his big hand on my back, whereupon I swallowed the whole chaw.

'I feel sick,' I said, the gorge rising in my throat.

'Come up to the fresh air. You'll feel better there.'

The place was starting to spin and I must have half-tripped because my uncle took hold of my two shoulders and pushed me before him along the iron landing, the deafening sound of the pistons in my ears, back to the hole and into the fresh air. 'You stand there for a minute,' he said, 'until you come round.'

It was so good to escape from the overpowering heat and feel the breeze on my face. I gulped the air into my lungs.

I still felt sick, however, and wanted mother; so I set out along the deck, walking carefully like a drunken man, colliding with people as I passed and they looking at me in astonishment.

I found the family at last. I don't suppose it took long but my feet were like lead and there was a strange heaving in my belly.

'Where have you been?' said father.

'Look at his shirt,' said Aunty Bet.

'What's the matter with you?' said mother.

My father got up from his straw chair. 'Sit here,' he said, 'and put your head between your knees.'

It was too late!

I saw the deck rising to meet me, the ship standing on its head and everything going dark.

When I came round I was sitting on the chair, my head between my knees and my father had his hand on the nape of my neck.

'He's surely not seasick and this river like a duckpond,' said father.

'It must be something he's eaten,' said Aunty Bet.

'Are you better, my darling?' asked mother.

Then I vomited over everything and over my father's shoes and Aunty Bet shouted 'Oh!' and pushed back her chair.

I was better after throwing up, a sailor brought me a glass of water and a bucket and mop to clear up the mess. And everybody stared.

When my father saw me beginning to perk up the questions started.

'Where have you been?'

'What have you been doing?'

'Did you eat anything?'

'Nowhere,' I said – 'nothing – no.'

'Well something has caused this,' said my Aunt Bet.

'Tut! Leave him be,' said father after a while, 'the main thing is that he has recovered. You sit still until we reach Trefriw.'

I didn't go to see the stack being lowered for the ship to pass under Tal-y-Cafn bridge, but just looked at the fields alongside us as the river narrowed and saw an occasional cow raise its head to stare at us and the sheep scattering for the furthest hedges. A large cormorant stood on a rock by the riverside, its wings spread wide in the sunshine, motionless as if it were on a coat of arms; and the seagulls wheeled about us like a retinue, swooping now and again to catch a piece of bread or cake which someone had thrown up in the air. I could see the ship's wake like the arms of some enormous letter V reproducing itself, lapping under the banks as the river narrowed adding to the constant erosion of the tides and the floods.

We didn't stay long in Trefriw for fear of losing the tide and finding ourselves on a sandbank in the middle of the river instead of at the landing-stage in Deganwy.

But we had time to walk along the quay, and there was a café there and a place that sold ice-cream and a wooden shop; an ideal place selling all kinds of things, sweets, fruit, toys, decorative dishes with 'A Present from Trefriw' branded on them in paint, and, of course, all kinds of materials from the famous woollen mill. But I didn't want anything despite all Aunty Bet's urgings. It was mother who said the wisest thing.

'Would you like a cup of tea?' she asked.

And we went to the café and I never had as good a cup of tea, hot and sweet, scouring my gullet of the taste of tobacco.

I was warned that I was not to wander about on the return journey, and we sat in a row in the stern of the ship with nothing to do but think.

Then somewhere about Tal-y-Cafn I asked suddenly, 'What's a half-brother, father?'

I felt Aunty Bet stiffen in her seat and draw in her breath.

'That man,' she said, 'he's got hold of him – poisoned his mind.'

'Poisoned his belly more likely,' said my father.

'Now then, Dewi,' he added, with a stern look in his eye, 'the whole truth, my boy. What happened?'

'Uncle Josh said that he was your half-brother, Aunty Bet,' I said, and the stunned look on her face made me fear that she would jump over the rail into the river, 'and that you were the last little arse in the nest, mother. What does that mean?'

My father turned his head to watch a seagull that was flying with wings outspread behind us, before starting to explain.

'Your grandfather lost his first wife, you see, and Uncle Josh

. . . ' He paused for a second, looked at Aunty Bet, and smiled, ' . . . is one of her children.'

She tossed her head angrily and raised her shoulders.

'Then he married a second time and had more children. Aunty Bet and your mother included. Your mother was the last one, you see, the last little chick. Do you understand?'

'Yes.'

'I don't. Why were you sick? What did you chew?'

'Tobacco,' I said bluntly, and was frightened when I saw how my father's face changed.

'Tell me everything,' he said, and I had to obey, I told him everything in detail.

He sat in his seat tight-lipped, his two fists bunched at his side, saying nothing.

Somewhere between Tal-y-Cafn and Conwy he stood up, still angry, and said, 'I'm going to have a word with Joshua Gruffydd.'

'Don't be hasty, David,' said mother.

'Hasty,' said my father, looking at her. I never knew before that mother, even, was afraid of him when he meant business. But I saw it in her eyes.

And my father walked with long, slow steps towards the bridge, and the hole and the 'No Admittance'.

I couldn't restrain myself for long. I leapt to my feet and ran after him, weaving through the people who were now preparing to leave the ship.

I soon saw him, one hand leaning on the 'No' in 'No Admittance', his body sickle-shaped as he leant into the hole. I crept quietly on tiptoe until I stood behind him. I had to hear what he was saying. I could tell from his lips, that he was talking to someone.

'It's an abominable thing to avenge oneself on the innocent,' said my father in his pulpit voice. It sounded like a verse. My father would circle the vestry floor during the mid-week chapel meeting and people would tell him their verses, to which he would respond occasionally with a verse of his own.

I saw my Uncle Josh in the gloom inside and unfortunately he saw me, too.

'Hello,' he said, instead of answering my father.

'Hello, Uncle Josh,' I said, 'I'm all right now.'

'The little one at least doesn't bear me any grudge, David Oliver,' said my Uncle Josh.

At that my father turned, looked at me, and smiled. 'Unless you become as little children,' he said.

That was definitely a verse. I had learnt it for the chapel meeting a few weeks before.

'Come on, Dewi, it's time for us to go ashore.'

He grasped my right hand and moved away.

I waved the other at Uncle Josh and winked at him.

'No Admittance' it said above the hole, but I had been allowed in without let or hindrance.

The Arrest

Emyr Humphreys

I

A short stocky man stood in the middle of a room lined with books. He was in his shirt sleeves. His clenched fists inside his trouser pockets pressed down hard so that the tough elastic in his braces was fully stretched. He shut his eyes and breathed deeply. When his tight lips expanded with the conscious effort of subduing his excitement, he looked pleased with himself. He opened his eyes. They were a piercing innocent blue. A beam of the morning sunlight caught the framed photograph of his college football team hanging above the door. He saw himself picked out plainly in the back row, his arms folded high across his chest a tight smile on his face, his head crowned with golden hair cut short at the back and sides and brushed back in close even waves. It was a head of hair to be proud of. A blackbird in one of the cherry trees at the bottom of the garden burst into a prolonged cadenza. His hand opened and passed softly over the trim white waves that remained to him, still cut close in the old style.

His wife appeared in the study doorway. Her grey head was held to one side. She dry-washed her long white hands and smiled at him winningly.

'I don't think they are coming today, Gwilym.'

Her voice was quiet, a little tremulous with anxiety and respect.

'Cat and mouse.'

His thumbs planed up and down inside his braces.

'It's obvious what they are up to. Cat and mouse. Trying to break my will. Trying to make me give in.'

His wife lowered her head. Her concern seemed tinged with guilt.

'Let him stew a bit longer. You can hear them say it.'

The room reverberated with his resonant nasal baritone. He was a minister who enjoyed the art of preaching. His wife's attitude of troubled and reverential concern urged him on.

'The magistrates were very polite. Very gracious. The narrow iron hand in the thick velvet glove. A month to pay. That month expired, Olwen, ten days ago. And still they have not been to get me . . . That's the way things are done in this little country of ours. It's all persuasion, moderation, compromise. As I said yesterday, an entire population is guided, herded like a vast flock by the sheepdogs of the communication media into the neat rectangular pens of public obedience. And we still don't realise that those pens are process machines and that we have all become units of mass government analogous to units of mass production: uniformed wrapped and packaged products of the state machine.'

She closed her eyes before taking a step into the room. Her hands spread out in a gesture of pleading.

'Gwilym, she said. You've made your stand. The congregation understands and admires you. That's something a minister can be proud of. Why not pay now and have done with it!'

He lifted a warning finger.

'I have forbidden any member of my congregation to pay my fine! I have made a legal statement to the effect that all our property, such as it is, including our little Morris Minor, is in your name, "Mrs Olwen Dora Ellis". They can come when they like to arrest me.'

She moved to the window and looked forlornly at their narrow strip of garden and the circular rockery they had built together. The aubretia was already in flower. The north wall of the chapel was faced with slates that looked less austere in the vibrant sunlight. The minister ran his finger lightly along a row of volumes on a shelf.

'The role of the church in the modern world et cetera et cetera,' he said. 'How readily we take the word for the deed. It's deep in our psyche. What we need is more preachers in prison.'

'Yes, but why you, Gwilym?'

The question was intended as a humble appeal: but she could not prevent it sounding sulky. He waved it aside.

'Yes but where are the young ones? You are a man of fifty-six, Gwilym. You have certain physical ailments sometimes . . . '

'Piles,' he said.

He spoke as one at all times determined to be frank.

'Otherwise I'm extremely fit.'

'It worries me. I can't bear to think of you going to prison for a month.'

'Twenty-eight days.'

'It really worries me. I don't think I can stand it.'

They both stood still as though they were listening to the uninterrupted song of the blackbird in the cherry tree. He wanted to comfort her but her distress embarrassed him too much.

'We've been over this before,' he said. 'Somebody has to take a lead. Our language is being driven out of the homes of our people and our religion is being swept away with it. We must have an all-Welsh television channel. That's all there is to it. That's what our campaign is all about. When words fail, actions must follow. Stand firm, Olwen.'

At last he moved closer to her and put his arm over her shoulders.

'Now what about a cup of coffee?'

II

It was while they sat in the kitchen drinking it, the police arrived. Mrs Ellis glimpsed a blue helmet moving above the lace curtain.

'They've come,' she said. 'Oh my God . . . they're here.' She stared so wildly at her husband, she could have been urging him to run away and hide. He sat at the table, pale and trembling a little. He spoke in spite of himself.

'Didn't think they would come today,' he said. The peremptory knock on the back door agitated Mrs Ellis so much she pressed both her hands on her grey hair and then against her cheeks.

'I've got fifteen pounds in the lustre jug,' she said. 'Do you think they'll take them, Gwilym, if I offer them?'

The colour began to return to his cheeks.

'They don't really want you to go. The prisons are too full anyway. I read that in the paper only a week ago. They're too full you see. I meant to cut it out to show you. They won't have room for you, when it comes to it . . . '

The minister breathed very deeply and rose to his feet.

'It's not a place for you anyway. Not a man like you Gwilym. This is your proper place where you're looked after properly, so that you can do the work you have been called to do. A son of the Manse living in the Manse. There isn't a man in the Presbytery who works half as hard as you do . . . '

'Olwen! Pull yourself together! Be worthy.'

A second series of knocks sent him rushing to the back door. He threw it open and greeted the two policemen with exaggerated geniality.

'Gentlemen! Please come in! I've been expecting you and yet I must confess I'm not absolutely ready to travel, as you can see. Won't you come in?'

He led them into the parlour. The room was conspicuously clean but crowded with heavy old-fashioned furniture. It smelt faintly of camphor. In a glass-fronted cabinet there were ceramic objects Mrs Ellis had collected. Two matching Rembrandt reproductions hung on either side of the black marble mantlepiece. The minister invited the policemen to sit down. The senior policeman removed his helmet. A dull groove encircled his thick black hair. Sitting in a low armchair he nursed both the charge-sheet attached to a clipboard and his helmet on his knees. His companion stood at ease in the doorway until he realised that Mrs Ellis was behind him. She recoiled nervously when he turned and pressed himself against the door so that she could pass into the room. He was a young policeman with plump cheeks and wet suckling lips. When she saw how young he was she looked a little reassured. The older policeman twisted in his chair to speak to her. His voice was loud with undue effort to be normal and polite.

'I don't expect you remember me?'

She moved forward to inspect his face more closely. His false teeth flashed under his black moustache and drew attention to his pock-marked cheeks and small, restless eyes. The minister's wife shook her head a little hopelessly.

'I am Gwennie's husband. Gwennie Penycefn. You remember Gwennie.'

'Gwennie . . . '

Mrs Ellis repeated the name with affectionate recognition. She looked at her husband hopefully. He was still frowning with the effort of identification.

'You taught her to recite when she was small.'

Mrs Ellis nodded eagerly.

'And Mr Ellis here confirmed her. I don't mind telling you she burst into tears after breakfast. When I told her where I was going and the job I had to do. "Not Mr Ellis," she said. "He baptised me and he confirmed me." Poor Gwennie. She was very upset.'

The minister nodded solemnly. He stood in front of the empty fireplace, squaring his shoulders, his hands clasped tightly together behind his back. The armchair creaked as the policeman lowered his voice and leaned forward.

'What about paying, Mr Ellis? You've made your stand. And we respect you for it. It's our language too isn't it, after all. I don't want to see a man of your calibre going to prison. Honestly I don't.'

'Oh dear . . . '

In spite of her effort at self-control, Mrs Ellis had begun to sigh and tremble. The policeman turned his attention to her, gruff but confident in his own benevolence.

'Persuade him, Mrs Ellis bach. You should see the other one I've got waiting in the station. And goodness knows what else the van will have to collect. The refuse of society, Mrs Ellis. Isn't that so, Pierce?'

He invited a confirming nod from his young colleague.

'Scum,' Pierce said in his light tenor voice. 'That one tried to kill himself last night, if you please.'

'Oh no . . . '

Mrs Ellis put her hands over her mouth.

'Younger than me too. Now he needs a stretch. Do him good.'

'Officer.'

The minister was making an effort to sound still and formal.

'This man you say tried to kill himself. What was his trouble?'

'Drugs.'

The older policeman answered the question.

'Stealing. Breaking and entering. Driving without a licence. Drugs.'

The policeman spoke the last word as if its very sound had polluted his lips. His colleague had managed to tighten his wet lips to demonstrate total abomination. He made a strange sound in his throat like the growl of an angry watchdog.

'Will you give me a moment to . . . dress . . . and so on?'

The policeman sighed.

'You don't need anything, my dear Mr Ellis. You go in wet and naked like the day you were born.'

Mrs Ellis moved into the crowded room. Even in her distress she navigated her way between the furniture without ever touching their edges. Her arms floated upwards like a weak swimmer giving in to the tide.

'I'll pack a few things,' she said. 'In your little week-end case.'

Her eyes were filling with tears and it was clear that she had not taken in the policeman's last words.

'Wear your round collar, Gwilym,' she said.

She spoke in a pleading whisper and made a discreet gesture towards her own throat.

'There's still respect for the cloth, isn't there?'

'I go like any other man who has broken the English law,' he said. 'Get me my coat, Olwen. That's all I shall need.'

The younger policeman looked suddenly annoyed.

'Look,' he said. 'Why cause all this fuss for nothing? It's only a bit of a telly licence. Why don't you pay the fine here and now like any sensible chap and have done with it?'

The minister looked at him.

'You have your duty,' he said. 'I have mine.'

III

The rear door of the van opened suddenly. The minister had a brief glimpse of men out in a yard smoking and enjoying the May sunshine: they were plain-clothes men and policemen in uniform. They paid little attention to the van, even when a bulky youth in frayed jeans was lifted bodily and pushed into it. He collapsed on the cold metal floor near the minister's feet. His large head was a mass of uncombed curls. When his face appeared his lips were stretched in a mooncalf smile. He was handcuffed and there were no laces in his dirty white pumps.

His wrists were heavily bandaged in blood-stained crepe. His nose was running and he lifted both hands to try and wipe it. A plain-clothes detective bent over him, still breathing hard.

'Now look, Smyrna,' he said. 'You promise to behave yourself and I'll take these off. Otherwise you'll be chained to the pole see? With a ring through your nose like a bull.' Smyrna was nodding and smiling foolishly.

'You've got a real minister to look after you now. So you behave yourself and I'll bring you a fag before we leave.'

His boots stamped noisily on the metal. The slamming of the rear doors reverberated in the dim interior of the police van. Smyrna, still sitting on the floor raised his arms to stare at his wrists. The minister nodded at him and moved to make room for him on the narrow bench. Smyrna's tongue hung out as he searched the pockets of his jeans for a cigarette. He found a flattened stump, rolled it between his dirty fingers and stuck it between his lips.

'Got a match?'

The minister felt about in his pockets before he shook his head. He looked apologetic. The young man sucked the wet stump. He lifted his bandaged wrists so that the minister could observe them.

'You know what he said?

'Who?'

'That sergeant. That detective sergeant. "Didn't make a good job of it, did you?"'

The minister leaned forward to scrutinise the lateral scratches ascending both the young man's strong arms.

'That's sympathy for you. I was upset. It's a terrible thing to happen to anybody. Eighteen months in prison. And that was all the sympathy I got.'

The minister gathered up the ends of his clerical grey macintosh and leaned forward as far as he could to show intense sympathy.

'How did you do it?'

Smyrna's lips stretched in a proud smile, the cigarette stump still in the corner of his mouth.

'Smashed my arms through the glass. Thick it was. Frosted. Too thick really.'

He mimed the act of scratching his arms with pieces of broken glass. Then he pulled a face to indicate his pain. The minister was distressed.

'Is it hurting now?' he said.

'Aye. A bit.'

Smyrna's head sank on to his chest.

The van lurched abruptly out of the yard. Through the small window the minister caught a glimpse of familiar landmarks warmed by the brilliant sunshine: boarding houses, a deserted slate quay, a wooded corner of the island across the sandy straits. Smyrna was on his knees communicating with the two policemen who rode in front. A plain clothes man the minister had not seen before, lit a cigarette in his own mouth and then passed it between the bars to the young prisoner. Smyrna settled at last on the bench, enjoying the luxury of the smoke, staring most of the time at the bandages on his wrists, lifting first one and then the other for a closer inspection.

The minister asked him questions. He wanted details of his background. As the van travelled faster the interior grew colder and more draughty. Smyrna's eyes shifted about as he tried to work out the ulterior motive behind Mr Ellis' probing solicitude. He pulled his tattered combat jacket closer about his body and sniffed continuously to stop his nose running. His answers became monosyllabic and he began to mutter and complain about the cold and the noise. His eyes closed. He sagged in his seat and his large body shook passively with the vibrations of the uncomfortable vehicle.

The van turned into the rear of a large police headquarters. It reversed noisily up a narrow concrete passage to set as close as possible to a basement block of cells. Smyrna jerked himself up nervously and called out.

'Where are we then?'

The minister tried to give a reassuring smile.

'I've no idea,' he said.

The van stood still, the engine running. There were shouts outside and the jovial sounds of policemen greeting one another, Smyrna's mouth opened and his eyeballs oscillated nervously in their sockets as he listened.

When the doors at last opened a smartly dressed young man jumped in. He wore large tinted spectacles and his straight hair was streaked and tinted. He wore his bright handcuffs as if they were a decoration. He sat opposite the other two, giving them a brief nod and a smile of regal condescension. There was no question of removing his handcuffs. His escort examined the interior and then decided to ride in front with his colleagues. As soon as the doors were locked the van moved off at speed. Smyrna unsteadily attempted to wipe his nose, first with the back of one hand and then the other. He stared at the newcomer's handcuffs with a curiosity that made him miss his own nose. His mouth hung open. A fastidious expression appeared on the new prisoner's face.

'You're a dirty bugger aren't you.'

A modish disc-jockey drawl had been superimposed on his local accent. The effect would have been comic but for the menacing stillness of his narrow head. It was held in some invisible vice of his own making. His eyes, pale and yet glinting dangerously, were also still beyond the grey tint of the thin convex lenses.

'I don't like dirty buggers near me. I can tell you that now. What do they call you?'

Smyrna's jaw stretched out as he considered the quiet words addressed to him. Was this a new threat forming itself? Had his environment become totally hostile? The well-dressed prisoner was handcuffed after all. He was a man of slight build. He looked down unhappily at his own powerful arms and began once again to examine the bandages on his wrists.

'Smyrna,' he said. 'Smyrna. That's what they call me.'

'What's that for Christ's sake. Some bloody Welsh chapel, or something?'

He bared the bottom of his immaculate teeth in an unfriendly smile.

'Now look here . . . '

The minister felt obliged to intervene.

'You must understand that our young friend here isn't at all well. You can see for yourself.'

The cold eyes shifted to examine the minister for the first time.

'Who the hell are you? His old dad or something?'

He directed the same question to Smyrna with the slightest nod towards the minister. He was amused by his own remarks.

'Your old dad, is he? Come for the ride?'

The minister made an appeal for sociability.

'Now look here,' he said. 'We are all in the same boat. In the same van anyway. Let us make an effort to get on together, and help each other.'

The handcuffed man studied the minister with the absorbed but objective interest of an ornithologist examining a known if unfamiliar species in a wholly inappropriate habitat.

'How long you in for, Moses?'

'A month. Twenty eight days that is.'

The minister was prepared to be relaxed and jovial.

'Oh dearie me. That's a very long time isn't it? What about you snotty Smyrna?'

'Eighteen months.'

Smyrna's large head sank on his chest. His jaw began to work. In the depth of his misery he seemed unaware of a trickle of mucus that ran from his nostril over the edge of his upper lip.

'Wipe your snot, you dirty bugger.'

The handcuffed prisoner's voice rose sharply to assert itself above the noise of the engine taking a hill in low gear.

'I bet you're one of those miserable sods who grind their

bloody teeth in their sleep. Aren't you?'

Smyrna smiled rather foolishly. He had no defence except to try and be friendly.

'How long you in for then?'

He put the question with amiable innocence and waited patiently for an answer. A pulse began to beat visibly in the handcuffed man's tightened jaws.

'Nine.'

He spoke at last, but so quietly Smyrna leaned forward as though he were about to complain he hadn't heard. One of the police escort shifted in his cramped seat to peer back at them through the steel bars. The scream of the engine subsided a little.

'Nine months did you say?'

Smyrna was smiling inanely.

'Nine fucking years you snotty piece of crap. If they can hold me.'

He lifted his handcuffed hands to the breast pocket of his smart suit and let them fall again.

'Here . . . '

He was ordering Smyrna to extract a packet of cigarettes from the pocket. Smyrna glanced apprehensively at the broad backs of the policemen in front.

'Never mind them, snotty. When you're inside you do as I tell you. You may as well start now.'

Smyrna was permitted a cigarette himself. He was instructed to sit alongside his new master to enjoy it.

'You sit there mate, and then I won't have to bloody look at you.'

Smyrna settled down, inhaling deeply and giggling. He blew on the end of the cigarette and pointed it at Mr Ellis.

'He's a minister,' he said.

'Is he now? Well, well. He should be sorry for us.'

He held out his handcuffed wrists and nudged Smyrna to do the same. When he understood the order, Smyrna shook so much with silent giggles that he had difficulty in keeping his bandaged wrists level and close to the handcuffs.

'We make a pair. A pair of Jacks. Isn't that so, Snotty? A pair of Jacks.'

Smyrna laughed delightedly. He let his arms drop but a glance from his new companion made him raise them again.

'What is it then. What is it you're in for?'

The minister cleared his throat. He straightened his back.

'For refusing to buy my television licence,' he said. 'On principle.'

'Oh my God. One of them language fanatics. I tell you what I'd do, Moses, if I was in charge. I'd stick the bloody lot of you up against a wall . . . '

'You don't understand,' the minister said. 'I'm not blaming you. You've never had a chance to understand.'

'Do you hear that?'

The man in handcuffs elbowed Smyrna again to show him he could lower his arms if he wanted to since he had decided the joke was over.

'He's a fucking Welsh hero. That's what he is. In for twenty days and then out for a fucking laurel crown made of leeks. That's him. I tell you what we'll do, snotty. We'll be in the same cell tonight. And I won't be wearing my bracelets. How about knitting him a nice little crown of thorns?'

Smyrna inhaled cigarette smoke to the bottom of his lungs and nodded gleefully.

The Return

Brenda Chamberlain

It isn't as if the Captain took reasonable care of himself, said the postmaster.

No, she answered. She was on guard against anything he might say.

A man needs to be careful with a lung like that, said the postmaster.

Yes, she said. She waited for sentences to be laid like baited traps. They watched one another for the next move. The man lifted a two-ounce weight from the counter and dropped it with fastidious fingers into the brass scale. As the tray fell, the woman sighed. A chink in her armour. He breathed importantly and spread his hands on the counter. From pressure on the palms, dark veins stood up under the skin on the backs of his hands. He leaned his face to the level of her eyes. Watching him, her mouth fell slightly open.

The Captain's lady is very nice indeed; Mrs Morrison is a charming lady. Have you met his wife, Mrs Ritsin?

No, she answered; she has not been to the Island since I came. She could not prevent a smile flashing across her eyes at her own stupidity. Why must she have said just that, a ready-made sentence that could be handed on without distortion. She has not been to the Island since I came. Should she add: no doubt she will be over soon; then I shall have the pleasure of meeting her? The words would not come. The postmaster lodged the sentence carefully in his brain to be retailed to the village.

They watched one another. She, packed with secrets behind that innocent face, damn her, why couldn't he worm down the secret passages of her mind? Why had she come here in the first place, this Mrs Ritsin? Like a doll, so small and delicate, she made you want to hit or pet her, according to your nature. She walked with small strides, as if she owned the place, as if she was on equal terms with man and the sea. Her eyes disturbed something in his nature that could not bear the light. They were large; they looked farther than any other eyes he had seen. They shone with a happiness that he thought indecent in the circumstances.

Everyone knew, the whole village gloated and hummed over the fact that Ceridwen had refused to live on the Island and that she herself was a close friend of Alec Morrison. But why, she asked herself, why did she let herself fall into their cheap traps? The sentence would be repeated almost without a word being altered, but the emphasis, O my God, the stressing of the I, to imply a malicious woman's triumph. But all this doesn't really matter, she told herself, at least it won't once I am back there. The Island. She saw it float in front of the postmaster's face. The rocks were clear and the hovering, wind-swung birds; she saw them clearly in front of the wrinkles and clefts on his brow and chin. He coughed discreetly and shrugged with small deprecatory movements of the shoulders. He wished she would not stare at him as if he was a wall or invisible. If she was trying to get at his secrets she could try till crack of doom. All the same. As a precautionary measure he slid aside and faced the window.

Seems as though it will be too risky for you to go back this evening, he said; there's a bit of fog about. You'll be stopping the night in Porthbychan?

– and he wouldn't let her go on holiday in the winter: said, if she did, he'd get a concubine to keep him warm, and he meant it.

A woman was talking to her friend outside the door.

You cannot possibly cross the Race alone in this weather, Mrs Ritsin, persisted the postmaster.

I must get back tonight, Mr Davies.

He sketched the bay with a twitching arm, as if to say: I have bound the restless wave. He became confidential, turning to stretch across the counter.

My dear Mrs Ritsin, no woman has ever before navigated these waters. Why, even on a calm day the Porthbychan fishers will not enter the Race. Be warned, dear lady. Imagine my feelings if you were to be washed up on the beach here.

Bridget Ritsin said, I am afraid it is most important that I should get back tonight, Mr Davies.

Ann Pritchard from the corner house slid from the glittering evening into the shadows of the post office. She spoke out of the dusk behind the door. It isn't right for a woman to ape a man, doing a man's work.

Captain Morrison is ill. He couldn't possibly come across today. That is why I'm in charge of the boat, Bridget answered.

Two other women had slipped in against the wall of the shop. Now, four pairs of eyes bored into her face. With sly insolence the women threw ambiguous sentences to the postmaster, who smiled as he studied the grain in the wood of his counter. Bridget picked up a bundle of letters and turned to go. The tide will be about right now, she said. Good evening, Mr Davies. Be very, very careful, Mrs Ritsin, and remember me to the Captain.

Laughter followed her into the street. It was like dying in agony, while crowds danced and mocked. O, my darling, my darling over the cold waves. She knew that while she was away he would try to do too much about the house. He would go to the well for water, looking over the fields he lacked strength to drain. He would be in the yard, chopping sticks. He would cough and spit blood. It isn't as if the Captain took reasonable care of himself. When he ran too hard, when he moved anything heavy and lost his breath, he only struck his chest and cursed: blast my lung. Alec dear, you should not run so fast up the mountain. He never heeded her. He had begun to spit blood.

By the bridge over the river, her friend Griff Owen was leaning against the side of a motor-car, talking to a man and woman in the front seats. He said to them, ask her, as she came past.

Excuse me, Miss, could you take us over to see the Island?

I'm sorry, she said, there's a storm coming up. It wouldn't be possible to make the double journey.

They eyed her, curious about her way of life.

Griff Owen, and the grocer's boy carrying two boxes of provisions, came down to the beach with her.

I wouldn't be you; going to be a dirty night, said the man.

The waves were chopped and the headland was vague with hanging cloud. The two small islets in the bay were behind curtains of vapour. The sea was blurred and welcomeless. To the Island, to the Island. Here in the village, you opened a door: laughter and filthy jokes buzzed in your face. They stung and blinded. O my love, be patient, I am coming back to you, quickly, quickly, over the waves.

The grocer's boy put down the provisions on the sand near the tide edge. Immediately a shallow pool formed round the bottoms of the boxes.

Wind seems to be dropping, said Griff.

Yes, but I think there will be fog later on, she answered, sea fog. She turned to him. Oh, Griff, you are always so kind to me. What would we do without you?'

He laid a hand on her shoulder. Tell me, how is the Captain feeling in himself? I don't like the thought of him being so far from the doctor.

The doctor can't do very much for him. Living in the clean air from the sea is good. These days he isn't well, soon he may be better. Don't worry, he is hanging on to life and the Island. They began to push the boat down over rollers towards the water. Last week Alec had said quite abruptly as he was stirring the boiled potatoes for the ducks: at least, you will have this land if I die.

At least, I have the Island.

Well, well, said the man, making an effort to joke; tell the Captain from me that I'll come over to see him if he comes for me himself. Tell him I wouldn't trust my life to a lady, even though the boat has got a good engine and knows her way home.

He shook her arm: you are a stout girl.

Mr Davies coming down, said the boy, looking over his shoulder as he heaved on the side of the boat. The postmaster came on to the beach through the narrow passage between the hotel and the churchyard. His overcoat flapped round him in the wind. He had something white in his hand. The boat floated; Bridget waded out and stowed away her provisions and parcels. By the time she had made a second journey Mr Davies was at the water's edge.

Another letter for you, Mrs Ritsin, he said. Very sorry, it had got behind the old-age-pension books. He peered at her, longing to know what was in the letter, dying to find out what her feelings would be when she saw the handwriting. He had already devoured the envelope with his eyes, back and front, reading the postmark and the two sentences written in pencil at the back. He knew it was a letter from Ceridwen to her husband.

A letter for the Captain, said the postmaster, and watched her closely.

Thank you. She took it, resisting the temptation to read the words that caught her eye on the back of the envelope. She put it away in the large pocket of her oilskin along with the rest.

The postmaster sucked in his cheeks and mumbled something. So Mrs Morrison will be back here soon, he suddenly shot at her. Only the grocer's boy, whistling as he kicked the shingle, did not respond to what he said. Griff looked from her to the postmaster, she studied the postmaster's hypocritical smile. Her head went up, she was able to smile: oh, yes, of course. Mrs Morrison is sure to come over when the weather is better. What did he know, why should he want to know?

It was like a death; every hour that she had to spend on the mainland gave her fresh wounds.

Thank you, Mr Davies. Good-bye Griff, see you next week if the weather isn't too bad. She climbed into the motorboat and weighed anchor. She bent over the engine and it began to live. The grocer's boy was drifting away, still kicking the beach as if he bore it a grudge. Mr Davies called in a thin voice . . . great care . . . wish you would . . . the Race and . . .

Griff waved, and roared like a horn: tell him I'll take the next calf if it is a good one.

It was his way of wishing her God-speed. Linking the moment's hazard to the safety of future days.

She waved her hand. The men grew small; they and the gravestones of blue and green slate clustered round the medieval church at the top of the sand. The village drew into itself, fell into perspective against the distance mountains.

It was lonely in the bay. She took comfort from the steady throbbing of the engine. She drew Ceridwen's letter from her pocket. She read: if it is *very* fine, Auntie Grace and I will come over next week-end. Arriving Saturday tea-time Porthbychan. Please meet.

Now she understood what Mr Davies had been getting at. Ceridwen and the aunt. She shivered suddenly and felt the flesh creeping on her face and arms. The sea was bleak and washed of colours under the shadow of a long roll of mist that stretched from the level of the water almost to the sun. It was nine o'clock in the evening. She should not reach the anchorage before ten and, though it was summertime, darkness would have fallen before she reached home. She hoped Alec's dog would be

68

looking out for her on the headland.

The wind blew fresh, but the wall of mist did not seem to move at all. She wondered if Penmaen du and the mountain would be visible when she rounded the cliffs into the Race. Soon now she should be able to see the Island mountain. She knew every Islandman would sooner face a storm than fog.

So Ceridwen wanted to come over, did she? For the weekend, and with the aunt's support. Perhaps she had heard at last that another woman was looking after her sick husband that she did not want but over whom she was jealous as a tigress. The week-end was going to be merry hell. Bridget realized that she was very tired.

The mainland, the islets, the cliff-top farms of the peninsula fell away. Porpoise rolling offshore towards the Race made her heart lift for their companionship.

She took a compass-bearing before she entered the white silence of the barren wall of fog. Immediately she was both trapped and free. Trapped because it was still daylight and yet she was denied sight, as if blindness had fallen, not blindness where everything is dark, but blindness where eyes are filled with vague light and they strain helplessly. Is it that I cannot see, is this blindness? The horror was comparable to waking on a black winter night and being unable to distinguish anything, until in panic she thought, has my sight gone? And free because the mind could build images on walls of mist, her spirit could lose itself in tunnels of vapour.

The sound of the motor-boat's engine was monstrously exaggerated by the fog. Like a giant heart it pulsed: thump, thump. There was a faint echo, as if another boat, a ghost ship, moved near by. Her mind had too much freedom in these gulfs.

The motor-boat began to pitch like a bucking horse. She felt depth upon depth of water underneath the boards on which her feet were braced. It was the Race. The tide poured across her course. The brightness of cloud reared upward from the water's face. Not that it was anywhere uniform in density; high up there would suddenly be a thinning, a tearing apart of vapour with a wan high blue showing through, and once the jaundiced, weeping sun was partly visible, low in the sky, which told her that she was still on the right bearing. There were grey-blue caverns of shadow that seemed like patches of land, but they were effaced in new swirls of cloud, or came about her in imprisoning walls, tunnels along which the boat moved only to find nothingness at the end. Unconsciously, she had gritted her teeth when she ran into the fog-bank. Her tension remained. Two ghosts were beside her in the boat, Ceridwen, in a white fur coat, was sitting amidships and facing her, huddled together, cold and unhappy in the middle of the boat, her knees pressed against the casing of the engine. Alec's ghost sat in the bows. As a figurehead he leaned away from her, his face half lost in opaque cloud.

I will get back safely, I will get home, she said aloud, looking ahead to make the image of Ceridwen fade. But the phantom persisted; it answered her spoken thought.

No, you'll drown, you won't ever reach the anchorage. The dogfish will have you.

I tell you I can do it. He's waiting for me, he needs me.

Alec turned round, his face serious. When you get across the Race, if you can hear the foghorn, he said quietly, you are on the wrong tack. If you can't hear it, you're all right; it means you are cruising safely along the foot of the cliffs . . . When you get home, will you come to me, be my little wife?

Oh, my dear. she answered, I could weep or laugh that you ask me now, here. Yes, if I get home.

Soon you'll be on the cold floor of the sea, said Ceridwen.

Spouts of angry water threatened the boat that tossed sideways. Salt sprays flew over her.

Careful, careful, warned Alec. We are nearly on Pen Cader, the rocks are near now, we are almost out of the Race.

A seabird flapped close to her face, then with a cry swerved away, its claws pressed backwards.

Above the noise of the engine there was now a different sound, that of water striking land. For an instant she saw the foot of a black cliff. Wet fangs snapped at her. Vicious fangs, how near they were. Shaken by the sight, by the rock death that waited, she turned the boat away from the Island. She gasped as she saw white spouting foam against the black and slimy cliff. She was once more alone. Alec and Ceridwen, leaving her to the sea, had been sucked into the awful cloud, this vapour without substance or end. She listened for the foghorn. No sound from the lighthouse. A break in the cloud above her head drew her eyes. A few yards of the mountaintop of the Island was visible, seeming impossibly high, impossibly green and homely. Before the eddying mists rejoined, she saw a thin shape trotting across the steep grass slope, far, far up near the crest of the hill. Leaning forward, she said aloud: O look, the dog. It was Alec's dog keeping watch for her. The hole in the mist closed up, the shroud fell thicker than ever. It was terrible, this loneliness, this groping that seemed as if it might go on for ever.

Then she heard the low-throated horn blaring into the fog. It came from somewhere on her right hand. So in avoiding the rocks she had put out too far to sea and had overshot the anchorage. She must be somewhere off the southern headland near the pirate's rock. She passed a line of lobster floats.

She decided to stop the engine and anchor where she was, hoping that the fog would clear at nightfall. Then she would be able to return on to her proper course. There was an unnatural silence after she had cut off the engine. Water knocked against the boat.

Cold seeped into her bones from the planks. With stiff wet hands she opened the bag of provisions, taking off the crust of a loaf and spreading butter on it with her gutting knife. As she ate, she found that for the first time in weeks she had leisure in which to review her life. For when she was on the farm it was eat, work, sleep, eat, work, sleep, in rotation.

I have sinned or happiness is not for me, she thought. It was her heart's great weakness that she could not rid herself of superstitious beliefs.

Head in hands, she asked: But how have I sinned? I didn't steal another woman's husband. They had already fallen apart when I first met Alec. Is too great happiness itself a sin? Surely it's only because I am frightened of the fog that I ask, have I sinned, is this my punishment? When the sun shines I take happiness with both hands. Perhaps it's wrong to be happy when half the people of the world are chainbound and hungry, cut off from the sun. If you scratch below the surface of most men's minds you find that they are bleeding inwardly. Men want to destroy themselves. It is their only hope. Each one secretly nurses the death-wish, to be god and mortal in one; not to die at nature's order, but to cease on his own chosen day. Man has destroyed so much that only the destruction of all life will satisfy him.

How can it be important whether I am happy or unhappy? And yet it's difficult for me to say. I am only one, what does my fate matter? For I want to be fulfilled like other women. What have I done to be lost in winding sheets of fog?

And he will be standing in the door wondering that I do not come.

For how long had she sat in the gently rocking boat? It was almost dark and her eyes smarted from constant gazing. Mist weighed against her eyeballs. She closed her eyes for relief.

Something was staring at her. Through drawn lids she felt the steady glance of a sea-creature. She looked at the darkening waves. Over an area of a few yards she could see; beyond, the wave was cloud, the cloud was water. A dark, wet-gleaming thing on the right. It disappeared before she could make out what it was. And then, those brown beseeching eyes of the seal cow. She had risen near by, her mottled head scarcely causing a ripple. Lying on her back in the grey-green gloom of the sea she waved her flippers now outwards to the woman, now inwards to her white breast, saying, come to me, come to me, to the caverns where shark bones lie like tree trumps, bleached, growth-ringed like trees.

Mother seal, seal cow. The woman stretched out her arms. The attraction of those eyes was almost strong enough to draw her to salt death. The head disappeared. The dappled back turned over in the opaque water, and dived. Bridget gripped the side of the boat, praying that this gentle visitant should not desert her.

Hola, hola, hola, seal mother from the eastern cave.

Come to me, come to me, come to me. The stone-grey head reappeared on the other side, on her left. Water ran off the whiskered face, she showed her profile; straight nose, and above, heavy lids drooping over melancholy eyes. When she plunged, showing off her prowess, a sheen of pearly colours ran over the sleek body.

They watched one another until the light failed to penetrate the fog. After the uneasy summer twilight had fallen, the woman was still aware of the presence of the seal. She dozed off into a shivering sleep through which she heard faintly the snorting of the sea creature. A cold, desolate sound. Behind that again was the bull-throated horn bellowing into the night.

She dreamed: Alec was taking her up the mountain at night under a sky dripping with blood. Heaven was on fire. Alec was gasping for breath. The other islanders came behind, their long shadows stretching down the slope. The mountain top remained far off. She never reached it.

Out of dream, she swam to consciousness, painfully leaving the dark figures of fantasy. A sensation of swimming upwards through fathoms of water. The sea of her dreams was dark and at certain levels between sleeping and waking a band of light ran across the waves. Exhaustion made her long to fall back to the sea-floor of oblivion, but the pricking brain floated her at last on to the surface of morning.

She awoke with a great wrenching gasp that flung her against the gunwale. Wind walked the sea. The fog had gone, leaving the world raw and disenchanted in the false dawn. Already, gulls were crying for a new day. Wet and numb with cold, the woman looked about her. At first it was impossible to tell off what shore the boat was lying. For a few minutes it was enough to know that she was after all at anchor so close to land.

Passing down the whole eastern coastline, she had rounded the south end and was a little way past Mallt's bay on the west. The farmhouse, home, seemed near across the foreshortened fields. Faint light showed in the kitchen window, a warm glow in the grey landscape. It was too early for the other places, Goppa, Pen Isaf, to show signs of life. Field, farm, mountain, sea and sky. What a simple world. And below the undercurrents.

Mechanically she started up the engine and raced round to the anchorage through mounting sea spray and needles of rain.

She made the boat secure against rising wind, then trudged through seaweed and shingle, carrying the supplies up into the boat-house. She loitered inside after putting down the bags of food. Being at last out of the wind, no longer pitched and tumbled on the sea, made her feel that she was in a vacuum. Wind howled and thumped at the walls. Tears of salt water raced down the body of a horse scratched long ago on the window by Alec. Sails stacked under the roof shivered in the draught forced under the slates. She felt that she was spinning wildly in some mad dance. The floor rose and fell as the waves had done. The earth seemed to slide away and come up again under her feet. She leant on the windowsill, her forehead pressed to the pane. Through a crack in the glass wind poured in a cold stream across her cheek. Nausea rose in her against returning to the shore for the last packages. After that there would be almost the length of the Island to walk. At the thought she straightened herself, rubbing the patch of skin on her forehead where pressure on the window had numbed it. She fought her way down to the anchorage. Spume blew across the rocks, covering her sea boots. A piece of wrack was blown into the wet tangle of her hair. Picking up the bag of provisions, she began the return journey. Presently she stopped, put down the bag, and went again to the waves. She had been so long with them that now the thought of going inland was un-nerving. Wading out until water swirled round her knees she stood relaxed, bending like a young tree under the wind's weight. Salt was crusted on her lips and hair. Her feet were sucked by outdrawn shingle. She no longer wished to struggle but to let a wave carry her beyond the world.

I want sleep, she said to the sea. O God, I am so tired, so tired. The sea sobbed, sleep, the wind mourned, sleep.

Oystercatchers flying in formation, a pattern of black and white and scarlet, screamed: we are St Bride's birds, we saved Christ, we rescued the Saviour.

A fox-coloured animal was coming over the weedy rocks of the point. It was the dog, shivering and mist-soaked as if he had been out all night. He must have been lying in a cranny and so missed greeting her when she had landed. He fawned about her feet, barking unhappily.

They went home together, passing Pen Isaf that slept; Goppa too. It was about four o'clock of a summer daybreak. She picked two mushrooms glowing in their own radiance. Memories came of her first morning's walk on the Island. There had been a green and lashing sea and gullies of damp rock, and parsley fern among loose stones. Innocent beginning, uncomplicated, shadowless. As if looking on the dead from the pinnacle of experience, she saw herself as she had been.

She opened the house door; a chair scraped inside. Alec stood in the kitchen, white with strain and illness.

So you did come, he said dully.

Yes, she said with equal flatness, putting down the bags.

How sick, how deathly he looked.

Really, you shouldn't have sat up all night for me. He stirred the pale ashes; a fine white dust arose.

Look, there's still fire, and the kettle's hot. He coughed. They drank the tea in silence, standing far apart. Her eyes never left his face. And the sea lurched giddily under her braced feet. Alec went and sat before the hearth. Bridget came up behind his chair and pressed her cheek to his head. She let her arms fall slackly round his neck. Her hands hung over his chest. Tears grew in her eyes, brimming the lower lids so that she could not see. They splashed on to his clenched fists. He shuddered a little. Without turning his head, he said: Your hair's wet. You must be so tired.

Yes, she said, so tired. Almost worn out.

Come, let us go to bed for an hour or two.

You go up, she answered, moving away into the back kitchen; I must take off my wet clothes first.

Don't be long. Promise me you won't be long. He got up out of the wicker chair, feeling stiff and old, to be near her where she leant against the slate table. One of her hands was on the slate, the other was pealing off her oilskin trousers.

He said: don't cry. I can't bear it if you cry.

I'm not, I'm not. Go to bed, please.

I thought you would never get back.

She took the bundle of letters out of the inner pocket of her coat and put them on the table. She said: there's one for you from Ceridwen.

Never mind about the letters. Come quickly to me. She stood naked in the light that spread unwillingly from sea and sky. Little channels of moisture ran down her flanks, water dripped from her hair over the points of her breasts. As she reached for a towel he watched the skin stretch over the fragile ribs. He touched her thigh with his fingers, almost a despairing gesture. She looked at him shyly, and, swiftly bending, began to dry her feet. Shaking as if from ague, she thought her heart's beating would be audible to him.

He walked abruptly away from her, went upstairs. The boards creaked in his bedroom.

Standing in the middle of the floor surrounded by wet clothes, she saw through the window how colour was slowly draining back into the world. It came from the sea, into the wild irises near the well, into the withy beds in the corner of the field. Turning, she went upstairs in the brightness of her body.

He must have fallen asleep as soon as he lay down. His face was bleached, the bones too clearly visible under the flesh. Dark folds of skin lay loosely under his eyes. Now that the eyes were hidden, his face was like a death-mask. She crept quietly into bed beside him.

Through the open window came the lowing of cattle. The cows belonging to Goppa were being driven up for milking. Turning towards the sleeping man, she put her left hand on his hip. He did not stir.

She cried then as if she would never be able to stop, the tears gushing down from her eyes until the pillow was wet and stained from her weeping.

What will become of us, what will become of us?

Deprivation

Eigra Lewis Roberts
Translated from the Welsh by Enid R. Morgan

As Lisi Blodwen arranged the tinned salmon for her tea, she
reflected that every old maid and widow should have a cat. Not
that there was any great pleasure to be had from a relationship
with an animal, but at least one could pet a cat or sulk at it
without hurting its feelings or raising its hopes. And a cat, thank
heaven, could not afford to sulk. On reflection there was more
and more to be said for having one. What would be the best
kind? A pedigree cat, perhaps, of princely blood; a cat to adorn
a hearth. But no; a true blue-blooded cat would need such
fussing. What a strain to have to treat a cat as an equal. No, a cat
without a family tree would be best, one that could be kicked
out of the way, and kept at a distance.

The salmon was good, so good indeed that she felt she could
eat it all at once. And why not? She could afford to be greedy
now, or lazy, or sluttish. She could afford to take the brake off all
her weaknesses. She decided to clear the plate. She was about to
settle down to it seriously when she heard the hard heels of her
sister Jane on the back cobbles. This was Jane's third call today.
Indeed, she'd been hovering around the house like the plague
for days now. Trying to reason with Jane two or three times a
day took all the strength she had. Every time she heard the

sound of feet in the yard her inside would turn to water and she would have to hurry to the lavatory. Jane's refrain today was that Lisi Blodwen should take down the photograph of Huw Llewelyn from the mantelpiece. It was useless trying to explain to Jane that seeing Huw's face on the shelf was the next best thing to having him here with her.

She pushed the plate an arm's length away. She was just wiping her mouth with her handkerchief when Jane stepped into the kitchen, rigid with authority. Lisi half expected to see her waving a search warrant.

'Having your tea?'

'Just finished.'

'Don't take any notice of me.'

'No, I've done very well. What about you?'

'I could do with a bite.'

'There's a plate of salmon.'

'It looks good.'

'I've just opened it.'

'I don't want to take your meal.'

'I don't want it. It's too much for one.'

'I should think so indeed. There's enough here for three.'

Blodwen watched her sister digging into the salmon. Little pink streams ran down her chin and she pushed a large tongue out every now and then to catch them. So that was the end of her salmon. She didn't have much heart for it now in any case.

'Clear the plate.'

'Yes, I might as well. It won't keep in this close weather.'

'Excuse me. I've got to go to the back for a moment.'

'Again?'

'People do go.'

'Yes – within reason. Really I don't know what I wouldn't like to do to that old man, hurting you like this.'

'You talk about him as if he were an old pig or something.'

'A pig has more respect for its sty than he ever had for you. I never liked the man.'

'I never heard you criticize him before this happened.'

'I didn't want to hurt your feelings.'

'I've still got those. Anyway, there's no point in scratching old sores.'

'Not on a corpse there isn't. That gets cleaned up quickly enough. But this old skeleton is still breathing. And he'll be back from his honeymoon soon, and that wife of his hanging on to him. The baggage that she is!'

'So she's catching it now?'

'She knew very well that he belonged to you.'

'I had no more right to him than she had.'

'After twenty years of courting? You'd better go to the back. I'll expect a bit more sense from you when you get back.'

Lisi Blodwen sat on the lavatory seat. Thank goodness for a place to sit down out of sight and sound of Jane for a moment. Really there wasn't anywhere better than the lavatory for relaxing and contemplating life's problems. She'd settled dozens of problems sitting here. Nothing to distract one, nothing but the sound of water snoring in the pipes. Two more days and Huw Llewelyn and his new wife would be back in town. The pair of them would be shopping in Tesco's on Saturday afternoon (Huw Llewelyn had had plenty of practice carrying those silly little wire baskets). They would be there in the cross-seats in Salem on Sunday night (one seat away from the deacons' row); they would be welcoming people to their house and be welcomed to others' homes. Would there perhaps be an invitation to Llys Arthur? It would be an awful job to stay in the front parlour without slipping out to the kitchen every now and again to keep an eye on the food. Perhaps that woman would need help in carrying the dishes through. She would hardly know how to put her hand on every dish. Let's hope she'll take care of the hot water jug, at least. Sixty years old and still without a crack. Huw Llewelyn's mother had bought it in the church bazaar for sixpence ha'penny. And the jug had outlived her. What a pity that people had to go, while things so easy to replace stayed on.

But it would be easier to endure being with the two china dogs and the big Bible in the front parlour than to bear the good-byes. Huw Llewelyn standing on the step of Llys Arthur with his arm round his new wife's shoulder, instead of helping his sweetheart to avoid the holes in the road between Llys Arthur and here, as he had done for more than twenty years. But there wasn't much danger of that happening. Thank goodness there was another way between her house and the town, and that she had refused to turn Methodist with Huw Llewelyn.

'Blodwen, are you ill?'

There was no peace to be had, even in the lavatory.

'Hurry up, will you?'

Where did they go on their honeymoon? But nobody would believe they were on their honeymoon when they saw Huw Llewelyn with his hair thinning on the crown. He never had had a crop of hair like some boys. But what he had he kept neat, and he combed it as often as a girl.

'Lisi Blodwen, I shall have to get a move on.'

'I'm just coming.'

She could see Jane in the window watching her cross the yard. Her face looked comic through the lace curtains, the blue of one eye through one hole, the red of a lip in another and a lock of untidy hair like a coconut shy crowning the lot.

'You didn't have to wait.'

'Thanks for the welcome.'

'I was only thinking of you.'

'It would be better if you thought about yourself. I've got a husband to bear my burdens. What will you do now?'

'You didn't have to bother about the dishes.'

'I only cleared away a little. You'll have all evening to wash them, won't you? Well, what are you going to do?'

'I've got enough to live on.'

'I'm not talking about money. You yourself, inside, is what's important. A thing like this could shatter you at your age.'

'I'll get through it.'

'Do you remember how losing her sweetheart wrecked Emma Hughes?'

'She was only a girl.'

'She had more cause to pull herself together. A pretty girl like her can bring the boys running. You've still not got rid of that old picture.'

'And I don't intend to.'

'People who come to the house will have a shock seeing him baring his teeth at them.'

'Nobody comes here except you and your family.'

'Ugh! Look at those eyes of his, tiny and slit like a china cat. What did you ever see in him, tell me?'

'Where did they go on their honeymoon?'

'Someone in the shop said they'd gone to the tip of Lleyn.'

'Aberdaron perhaps.'

'Yes, perhaps that was what they said. But the whole country's full of some Aber this or that. Didn't the two of you go there once when you started courting?'

'We didn't go farther than Pwllheli.' Quietly.

'Really? Well, you have made a mess of things. Quarter of a lifetime down the drain to a dreg of a man like that. You're on the shelf now, anyway, do you realize that? And poor mother died worrying she wouldn't live to see your wedding. How long ago is that?'

'Twelve years.'

'And you're still without a man.'

'That's a gruesome thing to say.'

'I don't know that it wouldn't have been better to have lived in sin than hold hands like school kids. At least you'd have something to look back on.'

'Yes, I would.'

'Twenty years of courting. Walking down Betws road, and enough room to drive a cart between you.'

'End of term meetings and the Sunday School trip.'

'And an occasional night at the pictures – home at eight.'

'A quarter past. Then we'd sit here for hours talking.'

'What about?'

'What does one talk about?'

'About rents and shop bills and the future for the kids.'

'We always found something to talk about. That was his chair.'

'As if I didn't know. Did you change chairs sometimes?'

'Never. We'd take our coats off in the lobby and then straight to our chairs. Huw Llewelyn that side and me the other.'

'Good God, and the bedroom above you. Tell me, have you got any glands?'

Lisi Blodwen felt a cramp in her stomach.

'I've got to go to the back again, Jane.'

'God save us. There won't be any of you left. Is it all right for me to go home?'

'Yes, of course.'

'I don't really like leaving you.'

Jane went with her to the back and stood at the lavatory door. Lisi Blodwen stood there too. There was something unseemly in opening the door in Jane's presence.

'Do you know where I could get hold of a cat?' she asked hesitantly.

'So it's come to that, has it?'

'Come to what?'

'That you've got to have a cat instead of a man in your life.'

'A cat can be a lot more agreeable than a man, so they say.'

'Well, it's not likely to take off and leave you on the rubbish dump anyway. And you can talk to it if you don't have anyone else to talk to. Do you remember how Auntie Dora used to be?'

'Who wouldn't?'

'She used to carry on talking to herself night and day; question and answer, just like the catechism. Yes indeed, a cat, at once. It's lucky that cats aren't so hard to come by as lovers. I'll call later if I hear of one.'

Lisi already regretted mentioning the cat. It wouldn't dawn on Jane that there were cats and cats, just like men and men. Jane wouldn't mind bringing along any old skeleton in tow. One of those creatures that skulk from wall to hedge at night, perhaps, with its fur full of fleas. It would be a disgrace to her hearth to let in a creature like that. Ugh, she had never had much to say for cats. But she could manage. Great God, she would have to manage.

She didn't have to go to the lavatory after all. Her inside steadied as soon as she said good-bye to Jane. She went back to the house and the kitchen. She looked Huw Llewelyn straight in the eye. It wasn't fair to judge people from the colour and shape of their eyes. Huw had old Ifan Llewelyn's eyes, and everyone testified to the fact that Ifan was as safe as the bank. And she'd never had any cause to doubt Huw Llewelyn. In fact his word was as good as a vow on the Bible. But it was a pity that he'd taken that woman to Lleyn, of all places. He must have remembered that little hotel he had fancied so long ago. 'I'll come here on my honeymoon,' he had said. There must have been a lot of changes in that hotel by now, but perhaps the inside would be like it was, old and solid, and its coolness like a balm on the flesh. She had lain the other side of the wall from her sweetheart, and the groan of his bed as he turned had sent the strangest shivers through her. She would have run to him had there been a welcome for her. She'd suggested it tentatively, but not tentatively enough to prevent shame from spreading in a blush on Huw Llewelyn's pale cheeks. 'We'll do everything properly,' he said. 'A ring first, and then bed; that's the way I was taught.' Of course Huw Llewelyn was right – cautious, wise Huw Llewelyn, the truest of men. She had done her best to be worthy of him.

Had he cooled towards her perhaps, after that night? But he'd courted her faithfully, without ever mentioning it. 'It would have been better if you'd lived in sin,' Jane had said. That's what she would have done. Jane was one to step first and look later. And Lisi couldn't remember her ever tripping up. And she herself, like a fool, watching every step. But she would have slept with him. One night in a little old-fashioned hotel, and the moon dangling outside the window, teasing them. One night she could have turned to now as to a book and read over and over again. On winter evenings with an empty chair opposite her, passing the summer night at the tip of Lleyn, lying safe and warm, shoulder to shoulder, thigh to thigh with her only lover ever.

* * *

Sometime in the evening Jane called again.

'Still sitting here,' she said sympathetically.

'There's no hurry.'

'Well I'm blowed. That picture's gone.'

'I put it on the fire just now.'

'You did a sensible thing, Lisi. The place is healthier already. I've got a cat for you.'

'What kind is it?'

'Just like any other cat for all I know. It hasn't opened its eyes yet. It will grow up with you.'

Splendid. She could put her foot down with it before it got cheeky.

'Don't give it too much room. I was thinking that perhaps that was what you did with that man.'

'Perhaps indeed.'

'Didn't he use to stretch out on the hearth as if he was the man of the house? But more fool you for offering him everything and getting nothing.'

'Nothing. When shall I have the cat?'

'The day after tomorrow if you like. They'll be glad to get rid of it. It would end up in the river otherwise. Not many people need a cat nowadays.'

Apart from old maids and widows, thought Lisi Blodwen. Especially old maids, for whom there was no point in looking forward or back.

'Damn that Huw Llewelyn,' she said aloud.

'Thank heaven,' said her sister Jane.

A House of One's Own

Siân James

I'm Liverpool really, proper Scouse, but I've lived here in Brynhir – Brynhir, Gwynedd, North Wales – for nearly three months.

I own this house, this garden and that little stunted tree by the back wall.

Plenty of people own houses, I know, but for me it's a near-miracle because I've never owned anything before, a bag or two of clothes, a box of kitchen stuff, that's about it really.

When I got the letter from the solicitor I was struck dumb for a whole morning. I wanted to shout out the news to Anna Marie and Gina and Scottish, Joe, the guys that shared the lousy flat I was living in ,but I had no voice, not even a Scouse croak.

I was the sole legatee, the letter said, of Mr Trefor Roberts, 12 Clydwen Row, Brynhir, Gwynedd, and I could, at my convenience, pick up the key to the said property from Jenkins and Hedges, Solicitors, Hill Road, Caernarfon, Gwynedd.

Mr Trefor Roberts was my uncle Trefor, my great-uncle Trefor.

I could just about remember him. He visited us once when I was small. I think he only stayed a couple of days, probably because our house was a proper shambles, full of lodgers and wet washing, but for years after he used to send my Mum a ten shilling note every week, fastened to his letter by a neat little gold safety pin, and that didn't half make a difference to our life.

My father, my real father, also called Trefor Roberts, was his nephew. He married my mother straight after coming out of the army in 1946, his boat docked in Liverpool and he never went back to Wales after. I was born in 1951, the only child. He died of pneumonia when I was about two, and a bit after my mother married my step-dad who was the only father I can remember.

My great-uncle worked in one of these local quarries, I don't know which one, and when he came to visit us – well over thirty years ago – he already seemed old. Perhaps it was the heavy black suit he wore and the shiny black boots. He took me to the Sally Army Hall in Toxteth Road and I remember how loud he sang too. I think that was the only time he took me out, but he must have liked me a bit to leave me his house. Or I was his only living relative most like.

I've been thinking about him a hell of a lot since being in Brynhir, though of course I never gave him a thought before. Here, sleeping in his bed with the lumpy green and fawn mattress, sitting in his sagging old armchair, eating at his little scrubbed table, he seems almost alive and I wish I knew a bit more about him. He's got a little shelf of books, but I can't fuckin' read them because they're all in Welsh – people speak Welsh around here. But he wrote his diaries in English, so I've been looking through those. I was quite excited to discover them, forty black diaries, Letts diaries, the sort with a little pencil in a groove at the side, all laid out in perfect order in the top drawer of his bedroom chest. Unfortunately they're totally boring, all about his work at the quarry, the times of the blasting and so on, and on Sundays, the name of the preacher at the chapel he used to go to, the text of the sermon and the grade he gave it, usually a B. I found myself longing for a really bad sermon, something to liven up his week, but there was never a D. I suppose he was always too ready to think the best of everyone.

The other day I walked past the chapel he used to go to. Several of the chapels around here have been closed down and used as warehouses or arts and crafts places, but his, Bethel, is still a chapel, and though I've never had a religious thought in my head, I was quite pleased.

Why should I be spending my time reading this man's boring diaries and thinking about him? I'm totally fascinated by him, that's why. If he was a cannibal chief he couldn't be more different from anyone I know; so quiet, so methodical, so tidy, so decent.

My next door neighbour, a cross old woman called Netta Morris, scrubs her step every day and when it's not raining I go out to see if she'll deign to speak to me. Usually she'll only mutter a grudging g'morning, but once or twice she's managed to part with a scrap of information. 'Mr Roberts was a good neighbour,' she said on one occasion. 'He always carried my ash-can out the back.'

'Why did he never get married?'

'He had no need. Could do everything for himself. Cooking, washing, ironing, even mending.'

'Didn't he need a bit of company? A bit of comfort?'

She went back into her house at that question, closing the door firmly behind her.

I've always needed lots of company, lots of comfort. My mother was the same, but I'm worse. I've always needed lots of men and lots of booze, but for three months I've had neither. Being a property owner in Brynhir has filled my brain so that I don't need anything else, but it won't last. One of these days I'll pick up my giro, go down the pub on the pull and fill the house with men and loud sexy music and to hell with Netta Morris.

Last week I bought a large, dark green waterproof coat which cost twenty-three pounds. I could hardly believe what I was doing. I've never before owned such a remarkably boring and hideous garment. Oh yes, I know it will be useful – it doesn't stop raining in this place – and practical too because it will hide all the tat underneath, but since when have I gone in for being dry and respectable? Perhaps it's due to losing so much weight; I'm almost human-shaped now, what with giving up the booze and the Chinese takeaways. I also bought a window cleaner called Mr Brite and some new bags for Uncle Trefor's old Hoover. Am I becoming a fuckin' housewife?

I've got to the 1959 diary and discovered that in March that year Uncle Trefor was faced with a problem. The owner of his house, a Richard Paul Mathias, died, leaving it to two of his cousins who are in dispute over the will so that he doesn't know who to send the rent to. In April he went to Caernarfon to take advice from a Mr Stanley Jenkins, solicitor, who tells him not to send it to anyone until the matter has been settled.

I'm in a cold sweat. Do the cousins of Richard Paul Mathias still own this house? Will I discover that this damp three-roomed terraced house – one room up, one room down and lean-to kitchen – is not really mine? I rush to the 1960 diary only to find that on January the first, my Uncle Trefor is still reporting that Mr Jenkins has advised him not to offer anyone the rent until it's demanded, but to keep the house in a good state of repair.

I'm too bloody agitated to read through the accounts of Sunday sermons and quarry blasting after that.

And it's that afternoon that the Reverend comes to call, the Reverend Dilwyn Owen, Bethel, a short, fat, jolly-looking man, about sixty years of age. 'I've given you plenty of time to settle in,' he says at the door, smiling a lot.

'I'm not one of the saved,' I tell him. 'I'm a big, bad sinner, I'm afraid. An alcoholic, for one thing.' Even as I say it, I realize it's not strictly true. I've hardly had a single drink in the last three months and when I went to The Bell last Friday night I only had two halves.

'Then you need friends,' he says.

I give him some brownie points for that. The holy joes

usually say they'll fuckin' pray for me. 'Come in.' He's the first person to cross the threshold.

'It's a tidy little cottage,' he says. 'Mr Roberts always kept it nice and you the same.'

'You knew him well? The old man?'

'No one knew him well, but I knew him as well as anyone, I think.'

'Sit down,' I said, pointing to Uncle Trefor's armchair. 'Will you have a cup of tea?' Three months in this place and I'm offering cups of tea to elderly men in dog collars.

'I'll sit and talk, anyhow. I had a cup of tea half an hour ago. I'm getting fat on religious tea.'

'I want to ask you something. Only it's not to do with God.'

'Fire away. It's the God questions I'm frightened of.'

'Did my uncle really own this house? I've been reading his diaries and it seems to me that his landlord's cousins are the real owners.'

'I can put your mind at rest about that. Mr Roberts owned this house. The court granted him the title deeds because he'd maintained it in good order and repair for over twenty years.'

'And that's legal?'

'Perfectly legal. I've got the facts at my fingertips because I often use it as a text for my sermons. It has a great moral significance in my opinion, who owns Wales, for instance, who are the rightful inheritors. But I won't bore you with politics. Suffice it to say, you own this house.'

'I'm very grateful to you. It saves me a trip to Caernarfon and a lot of worry.'

'There we are. What are friends for? Incidentally, do you know what Mr Roberts did with his rent money every week?'

'Used it to maintain the property, you said.'

'He did maintain the property, certainly, but that ten shillings rent he used to send to your mother every week.'

'I remember it arriving every week like clockwork. Ever after that time he came to visit us.'

'Do you know why he visited her? At that time? The only time he ever went further than Caernarfon?

'No. Do you?'

'He'd read in a Sunday newspaper, *The News of the World* it might have been, that your stepfather had been murdered by some drunken fellows outside a local public house and he thought he should find out how your poor mother was taking it.'

'How she was taking it? Do you want the truth? She was over the bloody moon about it. And so was I. And so were all his bloody mates. Sorry about the lingo, Reverend.'

'Your stepfather wasn't a popular character?'

'He was a petty crook, a drunkard, a wife beater and a child molester.'

'He molested you?'

'Yes. He molested me.'

'I think I'll have that cup of tea. Thank you.'

Why shouldn't I tell the Reverend the truth? Let him know something about the real world out there? Yes, I was sexually abused, Reverend, from the age of – what? Three or four? And this at a time when social workers and their like weren't on the lookout for signs of it. No, I never told my mother. Not because I thought she'd turn against me or stop loving me, but because he told me he'd kill me if I did. Oh, I remember the way he'd kneel over me, pushing his fingers into me front and back, pretending it was fun and that I was supposed to laugh. 'I'm tickling you,' he used to say. And then he'd get his big prick out and hurt me real bad and when I cried he'd say, 'Tell her and I'll kill you.' And when he got his trousers back on, he'd take a knife out of his pocket and stand over me, stroking the blade of it.

I was nine or ten when he was killed. Some neighbours from the estate and the pub got up a collection for my Mum and the day after the funeral we went on the train to a fairground at West Kirby and we went on the Big Dipper over and over again until all the money was gone, shouting out with terror and joy. I didn't tell that bit to the Reverend, but that's what we did. Joy, joy, joy.

My Mum was a big woman like me. She was around forty by this time and she drank a lot and had lots of men friends, but we had quite a good sort of life for the next ten years. Lots of rows and shouting, specially when I got to be thirteen, fourteen, and wanting my own way about everything, but lots of fun and rowdy parties and really great celebrations for birthdays and Christmas.

She died at fifty – cancer – and after that I took over where she left off, work at the factory Monday to Friday and boozing and men at the weekend. And all the men were rough and greedy and easy to hate. There was no way I could admire or love a man was there? The memories of being used and abused stay with you.

* * *

The bloody diaries seem to be all I've got. After the quarry shut down, he often left his weeks completely blank except for the Sunday sermons, always Bs. Then in 1986 he starts to write a chirpy little slogan for every week which shows he's softening up but they stop abruptly in February 1987. In fact the diary stops altogether in May 1987. I wonder if he went blind? Or lost his marbles? Who looked after him from 1987 until he died in March this year? Would Netta Morris be likely to tell me? Probably not.

On Friday I go to the corner shop for my groceries. 'This is the tea Mr Roberts liked,' the woman behind the counter tells me.

So she knows who I am. Nosey cow.

I ignored her and bought a different brand. But then I relented. 'Did you know him well?' I asked her. 'He was my great-uncle, but I only met him once.'

'He was a very private man. Didn't speak much to anyone.'

'Who looked after him at the end?'

'He was active to the last, chopping firewood, digging his garden, doing his shopping, chapel of course every Sunday. Didn't smoke or drink. Not much of a life. Wouldn't do for me, I can tell you.'

I looked at her with new interest. 'Didn't I see you in The Bell last week?'

'That's right. My girl-friend and I were hoping you might join us but you left without as much as a glance our way.'

'Will you be there tonight?'

'We're there most nights.'

'See you tonight, then.'

'See you tonight. By the way, do you play darts?'

'Only when I'm sober.'

'Ta-ra then. See you tonight.'

* * *

Things are looking up around here. My new friend seems lively enough. Perhaps she'll introduce me to some decent man and a whole new decent way of life. Huh! Perhaps we'll have a few jars and a laugh together anyway.

'You got a husband?' I ask her.

'Yeh, we don't get on. You?'

'No, I don't have that grief. Any kids?'

'Three.'

'I got three kids too. They took them away from me though. They're in this home in Moorfields.'

'That's awful. How did that happen, then?'

'Couldn't stop drinking, that was my trouble.'

'Gets you like that sometimes.'

'Got me like that. Couldn't stop it. Seem to have snapped out of it now, though. Practically on the wagon.'

'You've got something behind you now. Nice little house. Make all the difference. Try and get them back.'

'I think about it. But I don't know. They've been back that

many times. No one believes in me any more.'

'I believe in you, kid. I know how hard it is. There's lots around here know how hard it is, coping with life with next to nothing coming in.'

'I had a good job once.'

'They're wanting chambermaids in the Maesgwyn Arms. That's a good job.'

'I've got no references, though. Nothing up to date.'

'You won't need them. Just tell them who you are. Mr Trefor Roberts's great-niece. Everybody knew him. You've got it made. When you've got a job and a house, you'll get them kids back. How old are they?'

'The girl's fifteen, two boys, nine and eight. The girl's a bit of a problem, though, one way or another.'

'Course she is. So's mine. Mine's sixteen and she was a proper little tearaway. But now she's got a job up Llandudno way, country house hotel, living in, and she comes home on her day off, sunny as you like. You go and see about the job. Things will work out for you in this place, you mark my words. Have another drink.'

'Just one more then.'

The next morning I have a hell of a hangover and I'm quite pleased about it too. I had a good night out with a new friend and things seem brighter. Maybe I'll go to the Maesgwyn Arms and maybe they'll give me a job on account of my uncle's famed respectability and maybe I'll contact the authorities and maybe I'll get my kids back and maybe we'll manage, as he did, keeping things in good order and repair. For years and years and years. Being bored and bored and bored. Is that all there is to life? I'll have to ask the Reverend. I don't think he'll fob me off with fairy tales. I don't want to be respectable, Reverend, just half-way decent.

Netta Morris knocks at my door. 'You woke me up coming in so late last night,' she says, 'and all that noise. Your uncle never disturbed me in fifty years.'

'Pity he didn't disturb you a bit. I bet you were a good-looking lass fifty years ago.'

'You mind your own business.'

'You want a cup of tea?'

She thinks about it crossly and then comes in. 'Your uncle never asked me in fifty years,' she says.

'Silly old sod,' I say.

The Circles

Peter Gruffydd

Ellis Bryn leaned on his stick in the collapsing outhouse of his family's now derelict farm, *Ysgubor Fach*. He was bent, thin-faced, skin reddened from seasons of Snowdonian weather. His eyes were deep back under jutting eyebrows. Ellis's cap darkened with rain for he stood under the largest hole which neglect and time had widened in the roof. When he moved forward to stare intently round the skewed doorframe his greased boots crunched among bits of slate, rafter, dead nettle-stems. Then he could see the circles, their curved, cupped shapes: *Cytiau Gwyddelod* some called them, Irishmen's Huts. Ellis did not know if that was right nor did he care. As far as he was concerned history stopped at his grandparents. History was what you cared to remember, a stone's throw in your own memory. Anything outside that was a minefield of suspicious, uninteresting claims.

There were five hut-circles of bluish, lichened stones, half-sunk or standing proud of the short plateau halfway down the sloping field. A small commotion began near the middle. Soil tumbled, piled up, then a tiny, reddish snout emerged, queried, tested the air. Nearby, a sheep, fleece already beaded with rain, stamped. The snout froze, shot back down, left a patch of red, clayey earth glistening in the rain. Overhead two ravens flew slowly into the mists, towards the high crags where they nested. Sheep bleated, sought each other out, little troops of them moving single-file to thornbush clumps. Beyond the field's sloped foot were the houses of *Tremawrth*, chimney-smoke straggling into the drizzle. Beyond them a new roundabout and dual carriageway snaked, like looped, pale, wide bandages, towards the coast. Traffic was thin this early.

For Ellis the community was himself amongst a clutch of small farmers and untrustworthy villagers, all ready to take a behind-the-back advantage. He looked down the field onto the smoking roofs of *Tremawrth*. Sunday: a few would be in chapel, fewer in the short-spired church beyond. Ellis spat. His parents had broken with chapel and he had never attended since he was fifteen. The break had been something to do with a row about one of the visiting preachers interfering with his then thirteen year-old sister after the afternoon service.

Rachel had died long since, a spinster all her life. She and Ellis had quarrelled woundingly over *Ysgubor Fach*. It was now a ruin, half its useless, sodden fields sold off, raw new houses on them, each sprouting tv aerials, one a satellite dish. The builder had paid Ellis a good price, good enough to make him think of giving up his sheep flock and small beef herd. Yet what would a single man do with his time? Dim memories of warnings about idle hands, their wilful ability to be drawn to forbidden fruit, ensured he kept a smaller flock and two or three bullocks. Something to do.

Ellis hated the land. It was bad, sour, no good, gashed with slate and stone, pocked with marsh and now poisoned invisibly with fallout. He frowned as he remembered the meeting: that smarmy Johnny in a black suit, blue tie, flicking words like 'tolerance-levels', 'relative dose', 'no cause for undue alarm', 'no immediate compensation', 'becquerels' (What the hell were they!) off his tongue like a pony shicked flies away in summer. Smart young bugger! Wouldn't trust him as far as I could gob, thought Ellis, for the umpteenth time. He had left early. He had not cared what the others thought and he did not care now. To hell with the N.F.U.

The rain thickened. Ellis peered. Should've brought my double-barrel, he reflected, jaw tightening. It would have been more impressive than a walking stick. He scowled, squeezed the stick's rough head. Perhaps they wouldn't come? Surely not – not in this pissing downpour. Like a blown, breaking cobweb a grimace flickered then fell from his face. Let it pour – teach 'em! Who did they think they were anyway! Interfering . . . *interfering!* Ellis slashed at dead nettle-stems; bits of brittle stalk flew out of the doorway. There was a cough and clatter outside. Ellis poked his head out.

'Bugger off!' he snarled at the bumping, wet rumps of two ewes jouncing away from the outhouse. His voice was hoarse, stony, dry, like one not much used to utterance. Stupid bastards, sheep, cunning too; I hate them as well. Now, what about Brewster? Never see much of him, don't want to but lately the planning officer had been drawing me aside at meetings – Can't remember why I'm a member of that either. Something to do with *Tada*? No. Brewster wouldn't come. He wasn't a man for dealing with the public. Ellis nodded, grinned to himself, remembering Brewster's stubby figure and his uncertain temper. Ellis admired single-minded people. Where'd Brewster come from? He spoke good Welsh for a foreigner.

Ellis belched, bringing a taste of salty porridge and even saltier bacon to the back of his throat. Ach, horrible! Fishing a half-bottle of Johnny Walker's from his raincoat pocket he only hesitated a moment. Who cares how early it is? Down his soured throat the whisky swam, dragging away the saline taste. Ellis gasped, eyes stinging, blinked at the rain, carefully screwed the top on, hearing its metallic, lisping sound as it was turned home. He slipped the comforting, glassy weight back into his pocket.

If they don't come soon I'll clear off home. Catch my death, standing around. He leant on the rough stone wall, pulling his wet collar up. Bloody hell, he didn't feel too good at all. Dizzy and weak. What the hell was wrong? Pull yourself together man, he ordered, but his dizziness got so bad he turned, staggering, to the back of the outhouse where an old table covered in dank dust, webs and dead flies stood in shadow. He had just enough strength to sprawl on it before he passed out, stick clattering down among dung and broken slate. The table, shot through with woodworm, creaked, shifted out sideways towards the door but held the farmer's deadweight. Raindrops silvered down through the holes in the roofs, wetted the stick so that it shone. The breathing of the man on the table became sterterous.

This is it, thought the middle-aged lady at the bottom-gate. She dismounted, propped her bike under an overhanging hazel in the lane. The stone-circles that *they* wanted to build on – one house: to be followed by how many? Glancing from under the slick brim of her yellow sou'wester she saw the new houses in the rain. The Lego-land beginnings, she thought. Those people'd build on anything. What did they care about except a quick profit? She snorted quietly to herself, looking for the bolt on the new five-barred gate. Brand new gate as well – that would be from ill-gotten gains.

Mary Watcyn was petite, matronly, with prematurely white hair and rosy cheeks, forget-me-not blue, frank eyes. A casual glance would have slid over her, dismissed her as an older, old-fashioned looking person, perhaps noted the apparently sturdy good health. But a considered look would take in the steady eyes, a clear line to the jaw and mouth, the way she had of drawing herself up, straight-backed, when engaged in conversation. Standing near a fresh molehill beside the stone circles Mary puffed out her cheeks.

Was she to be the only one to face that bully-bureaucrat and his fawning assistant? She thought bitterly about the indoor enthusiasms of the Historical Society. Sometimes it was an effort to concentrate their minds. Five minutes' outrage at what their secretary revealed about the Planning Authority's, and the builder's rumoured intentions towards the stone circles, had not been enough to fire them to move their academic limbs out on a wet day. Let the secretary to it! The members leant on her too heavily. She shrugged. Not so much as a hen-hut would be built on here while she breathed. No sign of anyone yet.

Mary checked her calendar-watch. Rain soaked the lichened stones and grey-brown bracken stems. She moved to shelter beside a thorn and poured herself some tea from her thermos which was wedged into her yellow oilskin pocket. Sipping the hot brew while rain dripped onto her blue wellies, she gazed across at the greystone, blue-slate wreck of *Ysgubor Fach* farm. Might be a good idea to shelter in there, if this rain carried on. God knows how long she'd have to wait but she was glad to have arrived early; it gave time to sort out her thoughts.

Man's an idiot, thought Brewster, watching Jones fumblingly trying to lift the spare wheel from the blue Sierra's boot; a fat, fawning idiot. Has his uses though. 'Gerron with it, can't you,' he growled at the struggling Jones. There was something in the man which called out Brewster's Warrant-Officer, colonial past.

'Yessir,' grunted Jones, lugging the spare wheel almost at arm's length so as not to smudge his fawn raincoat. Prat, thought Brewster. He eyed the hills; rain. Reach them soon unless Jones hurried. He leant over, fished Jones's umbrella from the boot. Jones was fitting the wheel on gingerly. Brewster kicked at the punctured wheel lying on the lay-by gravel. Perhaps this was a mistake, coming out to meet protesters.

Brewster rubbed his bristly moustache hard. Couldn't remember a bigger mess for a long time. Somebody (a bloody mole!) was grassing him up from inside the Authority. Or could it be the Lodge? That taciturn recluse, Ellis Bryn? Hardly. The builder then? A loudmouth if he ever saw one. This was a cock-up alright – their plans openly discussed in public. Shitting pig-iron! Bet that Smart Alec woman from the Historical Society'd be there. *She* was a pain: Mary . . . Watcyn, that's it. Uneasily he recollected seeing that name in an old roll of prominent members. Something Watcyn. That could be, partly, why that woman, and the society she was secretary to, had woken up, squawked, made a fuss. He had to go; straighten it out. Said he'd meet them there Sunday in the hope few would come. Rain would help too.

In all his years in the Services, though sourly never higher than WO, in Malaysia, Africa and now, because of his ability to learn languages (Welsh had been easy), this backwater, Brewster had cultivated private arrangements. It had always worked but this time there'd been a slip-up. He hated errors. No need to explain things to the hoi-poloi. Announce, do it; over and done with then. Could it be *him*? He eyed Jones's wide back. Never – Jones was under his thumb. Wouldn't have dared, whatever the reward; owed Brewster his job. You bet.

'Done now, sir,' smiled Jones anxiously, standing awkwardly. '*Da iawn*,' Brewster drawled in his most patronising manner, wasted on Jones who beamed and sparkled, 'C'mon: we're wasting time.' Jones shut the boot. As they started out slowly from the lay-by it began to rain in earnest.

Near *Tremawrth* Jones slowed down even further, crawling along behind a long Landrover. 'Overtake!' snapped Brewster. 'Can't. No room, sir,' apologised Jones. Grumpily Brewster hunched down in his seat, watched the wipers, the back of the bouncing vehicle in front. Good God, it was turning up the long tracks to the fields in which the stone circles were! Brewster grimaced, a kindling fury rising in him. He hated anything public. He'd get to the bottom of this; heads would roll then. Oh yes! He'd throw the flaming book at them. Twitching his bowler he thought angrily, 'Nobody makes a mug of me: nobody'.

Looking round at the circles in the stony field, Mary thought about the planning officials. What sort of vision, other than one of ill-cloaked self-interest, lurked in such people's hearts? Her thoughts were broken by the sound of vehicles lumbering up to the gate below. Leading was a once-white, longbase Landrover, followed by a bright blue Sierra, a County vehicle if she ever saw one, but who was in the first? Despite her curiosity Mary felt discouraged. Why her? Shrugging a little she screwed the cup back on her thermos and stood staring down at the gate and tall thorn-hedge.

A woolly-hat bobbled along the Landrover's nearside, disappeared then the back-door opened, lengthening the vehicle. Mary heard resonant barking. A big red dog flew out, crashed onto the bonnet of the Sierra halted behind the Landrover, barked, scrambled skidding onto the Sierra's roof and, just as the door opened, flung itself sideways over the hedge, knocking off a bowler-hat which had suddenly poked out of the car.

The animal rolled over, bounded springily up then went bonkering round in circles, yelping and barking hysterically. 'Must be a young one,' Mary thought, fascinated. The woolly-hat reappeared, a voice bawled, the hat vanished again. When the dog crouched for a quivering bowel-movement, Mary saw it was a handsome red-setter, out of its highly-bred brain with free space. The squatting dog spotted the grey mounds of sheep clotted together warily in the bracken above. From squat it rocketed towards them, a turd lobbing over and behind it, falling to the soggy ground. Simultaneously, slithering figures arrived at the gate, yelling at the dog and arguing loudly. One, that would be Brewster, was in green wellies, and aggressively held a bowler. Behind him a shorter, fatter figure struggled with a mac and umbrella, getting both tangled round itself and in the gate.

The woolly-hat, face aglow with effort, burst, wet glasses glinting even from that distance, through a non-existent gap in the hedge, leaving tatters of red anorak flapping from crushed thorn-twigs. The figure fell flat. Reaching the sheep the dog pranced to a halt, barking ecstatically. Tensed, unused to a frontal approach, the tight group of sheep eyed the dog. Then the leading ewe made a break and they stampeded. The dog gave chase, fell over itself and raced hopelessly wide as the sheep repeatedly halted, turned, ran at tangents.

The small man climbed wobblingly onto the gate, plus mac, briefcase and half-open umbrella. Brewster, joined by a tall, thin person wearing a headscarf and long, woollen coat, furiously rattled the gate. The small man fell off. A hatless third figure wearing a donkey-jacket stepped forward and opened the gate easily. Brewster strode into the field, 'Like a Centurian' flashed through Mary's mind, brushing the bowler on his sleeve. The third figure and the woman followed, carefully shutting the gate. On its feet now, the woolly-hat and torn anorak came windmilling uphill, shouting, 'Charles! Charles! C'mere – Bad Dog! Shit – ' It slid, stumbled, recovered, ' –You! C'mere Charles!' Raising her eyebrows Mary Watcyn went to stand near the circles.

She knew the lad in the donkey-jacket: Ieuan, from Bangor now, though born in Anglesey. He did odd jobs and gardening for summer-cottage people, when he could get the work. And she knew Brewster. Her jaw squared as she watched him stump slowly towards her place. The planning officer was not built for climbing uphill. Miraculously the manic dog had been whistled then patted to submission by the woman, who carefully ran her long coat's belt through its collar. From a far corner the chased sheep, bunched together, suspiciously watched the intruders. Mary knew but did not need to know, Jones, Brewster's assistant. The others were strangers. Jones, panting along behind Brewster, had the umbrella up, trying to hold it over the smudged bowler bobbing and weaving in front. Mary's eyes sparked with angry amusement: the servant mentality, she thought contemptuously. No wonder Brewster rode rough over all opposition. She had a thing or two ready to surprise him. The officials reached her first, Brewster an unhealthy scarlet. He turned to Jones, ignoring Mary.

'Pap-ers,' the planning officer gasped. Jones fumbled with a portfolio of files wedged into the briefcase, umbrella clamped sideways under his chins, Brewster fidgeted, gulped air in the rain until the others arrived, the woolly man quite breathless. Ieuan avoided looking at Mary, slid his pale glance sideways, back towards the vehicle. The thin woman smiled hopefully at Mary. She had a brown, careworn face, built for silences; blonde hair lay lankly across her tall forehead.

'Hello,' she said, nodding shyly. 'Quite an entrance, wasn't it? Sorry . . . ' She trailed off. Her accent was Home Counties. 'Why, that is quite alright,' Mary answered, a little surprised and awkward. She looked down at the dog, which appeared stunned, red tongue slopped out, fur turning tweaky in the rain. The woman's ersatz leash ran from her woollen coat, still looped through one side, under the dog's collar and back. Looking up Mary caught the other woman's eye. They smiled at each other.

'I'm afraid she – er, he, isn't properly trained yet. You see, we had – er, it, only a week ago, just before we came up for a break, and – '

'I'm sure the lady doesn't want to hear all that, Madeleine. Bad dog, Charles!' The dog started and whined. 'Allow – ' A gust of wind cut him off and papers rattled between them, cracking in the air and rolling damply over the grass. Jones wallowed after them, abandoned umbrella reeling and standing on its head in the freakish wind.

'Krizzache,' growled Brewster, 'Pick 'em up!' With help from the others Jones secured most of the papers in his anxious hands. He proffered them to Brewster who swiped them aside with a muttered, 'Never mind that. Get rid of them!' Clearing his throat the planning officer glowed into the stone circles then, a smirk creasing his face, he talked at them, through rising wind and driving rain.

'Mi ryda'ni wedi cyfarfod yn y fan hon, sef Cytiau Gwyddelod, Caea Bryn, heddiw, i – '

Mary was quick; 'I don't think these people understand, Mr Brewster.' 'You could translate for them,' Brewster leered.

After a pause, Mary nodded. No need to put his back up.

105

Brewster, backed by Jones and the retrieved, wagging umbrella, plunged on. Over their shoulders Mary glimpsed a group of sheep halt by the outhouse doorway, dither, mill around a bit then trample in .She immediately forgot them. 'We're here today, to – ' she began, hurrying to catch up with Brewster's monotonous but pacy delivery. Luckily his Welsh was pedantic and long-winded so she was able to summarise – 'look at this land, needed for development of one house only, and to – assess – its suitability. Objections have been lodged by the local Historical Society, among others, who, nevertheless, were clearly informed – That's not true!' Mary's mouth snapped tight shut. She and Brewster lowered at each other. No point in making a hornet madder, she thought again.

'Please go on. I'm sorry,' she apologised, with ironic meekness. Brewster's eyes congested with fury. 'Well, you know the rest! Tell'em . . . but I don't know what their objection, if any, might be . . . ' he ground out in English, staring at the woolly-hat and his wife. New opposition, perhaps? Woman had an educated voice. Affrontedly the woolly-hat man began to explain.

'We're here, briefly, because we are concerned for the environment and – ' he indicated Ieuan, who gazed intently at the ground – 'we'd heard – ' Brewster interrupted curtly.

'Where juh live?'

'*Pant Eglwys Fach* – Why?'

'Holiday cottage? Second home?'

'Well, yes, but – '

'That's it then.'

'What is?'

'You're not residents, not concerned parties. There aren't any objections from you at our office. You shouldn't be here. This is private land.'

'We – Now look here! We – '

'No, you look. I – '

'I think that's enough, Mr Brewster. We're straying fom the

point. And we're all getting soaked.' Mary eyed Madeleine's dripping woollen coat which hung on the tall woman's frame like a sodden duvet. 'There is a right-of-way over this land for the public, y'know.'

'They're not standing on it,' Brewster said sullenly, caught out.

'It's hardly marked out with flags, is it?' Mary was getting very annoyed. 'Our objection, delivered to your office, copy to the builder, Sion Porth, and the owner, Ellis Bryn, personally by me, is to ask for a stay on planning permission, so that we can at least excavate some of this site *and*, if it is to be built on, then these circles should be preserved as an historic site. That's all, I think.' Mary smiled at him.

Brewster paled a little, his eyes narrowed, and his lower lip drooped showing a row of stained teeth. Just then Madeleine gave an alarmed cry. They all glanced across at her. She held up the chewed, dripping ends of the woollen belt.

'He's – gone!' exclaimed woolly-hat, grabbing up the belt-ends, staring at them as if the dog had hidden itself there. Necks craned round to search through the billowing rain for Charles. Sheep grazed or stood against walls, chewing the cud, and the rain, lifted by a strengthening wind, shawled over them. There was no sign of the dog.

In the outhouse the body on the table moaned. A sheep which had lain down beneath the table started up, cracking its bony skull on the mouldy wood. The figure half-lifted its head and shoulders then flopped back into the webs and dust. The sheep bolted out to join three others poised nervously in the middle of scattered slates and timbers.

'Rachel . . . ' The sheep trampled uncertainly at the strange, weak voice. 'Rachel . . . didn' . . . we didn', *Tada*. We didn' . . . don't! *Paid!* Don't . . . ' Charles burst through the gaping window and the sheep shot to the doorway in a jamming rush. The dog was berserk. Sheep piled over and under each other trying to get out. Their clattering scramble and the dog's booming barks galvanised Ellis. He hoisted himself up, still held in a blurry memory of red-haired Rachel, her red hair and white skin, and his father, snowy-haired, huge, rearing over them, leather belt swinging, where they'd lain in the outhouse, playing mothers and fathers. Ellis forced both eyes open then fell off the table, rolling among the frantic mass of ewes and dog. Tearing lumps of draggled wool from the sheep, the dog closed its jaws on one of Ellis's arms. With a roar Ellis stood up; the sheep heaved; the dog unfastened itself from Ellis, cowered back from the raging, swaying man.

'Good Lord,' said woolly-hat, 'What's going on over there?'

'Where your animal would be, Mister,' snapped Brewster.

'Charles! Charles!' Woolly-hat stared in horror as sheep bulged in the outhouse doorway. 'He must – I'd better – Stay here! Oh hell!' The man began running anxiously towards the commotion. He still had the champed ends of Madeleine's ruined woollen belt in one hand. Madeleine loped after him, veering sideways as her coat was towed from her body. Suddenly the belt came loose and her husband galloped free, belt flapping behind. 'Charles . . . Oh, Charles . . . ' said Madeleine sorrowfully, halted in the rain, coat hanging from one shoulder onto the ground.

'Perhaps you all belong to the same Lodge . . . ' Mary hissed wickedly to Brewster who was staring at the distant shambles. Mary's whisper spun him round, eyes drilling into hers momentarily before he looked away.

'Dunno what you mean, Miss.'

Jones had turned to stone and, and mute witness, was now unintentionally holding the umbrella over Mary.

'What else explains it, Mr Brewster? Delayed letters, the neat little set-up, the silences – what else? And what d'you take me for, eh? Eh!' Mary would regret her words later, she knew, but she was past caring. Let them all go hang, the trouser-rolling lot of them! She had seen something in Brewster's eyes which told her they were no mere rumours which had repeatedly reached her ears.

'D'you bring them here? That lot?' Brewster rammed a stubby finger at the stationary Madeleine and her running husband.

'Never seen them before. Ieuan must have told them and they decided to come, I suppose.'

'That'd add up. No good. His father was a . . . ' Brewster stopped flushed. Jones looked glassy.

'Lapsed member? Disgraced? A whistle-blower? What was it, Mr Brewster – Which? What dislodged – forgive the pun! – Ieuan's father from your cosy little circles!' Mary was in full spate. She felt alone, baffled and dizzily furious. 'One more of your evasive tricks and I could arrange a surprise for you and your – friends!'

'Is that a threat? Hear that?' Brewster addressed Jones who had suddenly started to fiddle aggitatedly with the umbrella; it crumpled over Brewster's head. In a flail of arms and groaning brolly ribs Brewster's purpled face briefly emerged. 'Krizzache – You asshole!' Hard on the heels of his accurate epithet came a barking, shouting pandemonium from the ruined farm. They turned to see the red dog blur from the door after the careering, scattered sheep, almost smash into its owner who somehow pincered the flying animal between his knees. In the outhouse doorway was a slight, swaying, capless figure.

'It's Ellis!'

'What!'

'*Iesu!*'

They began to run but Mary, slower off the mark, anger still washing through her, saw Ieuan slope off, muttering something about seeing to the vehicle. That made her even angrier. 'Brewster, Ellis!' she called, moving quickly after them.

'*Tada! Paid! Rachel bach . . . Ta-da . . . *' Ellis saw his wrathful father, Rachel's hair a red, wisping cloud where she knelt before the belt-wielding man, then blackness hurtling in on him as the tightening vice in his chest exploded. He tottered forward, opening his mouth to protest – *Tada!* – but jerked then fell unconscious into the arms of woolly-hat. A released Charles was caught by Madeleine.

'Good God. He's ill, I think. Do something!' Woolly-hat strained under Ellis's weight.

'Purrim down, y'fool – Down. Gently! Ellis? D'you hear me? *Ti'n nghlywed i, Ellis?*' Brewster knelt in the bracken by Ellis's prone body. '*Ellis* . . . Ambulance! Quick! Use the car-phone. Hurry, man, hurry!' Jones hustled off, palely obedient, to do Brewster's bidding.

'Has he . . . ?' asked Madeleine.

'Stroke, Mrs – er – he's had a stroke.'

'Oh . . . '

Woolly-hat broke the rainy silence. 'I think we'd better go. I mean, unless we can help . . . I think – '

'Yes,' said Brewster, not even looking up, 'Go.' Down below Jones was running back, hatless.

They went, the man taking his wife's arm, she glancing back questioningly at Mary. The sound of a racing ambulance siren came faintly from the clearway below and beyond *Tremawrth*. Mary could see it turning into the village's side-roads. She felt tears prick into her eyes. Why this? She wished she had not come alone to this sad, dank place. Ellis's face was paler than porridge under Jones's shaky umbrella. Brewster buttoned Ellis's mac round the still body. The woman had asked Mary something.

'What? Sorry . . . '

'I asked if you'd like a lift? We could drop you somewhere . . . ' Madeleine stared at Mary hopefully. Woolly-hat kept his back turned.

'What! Oh, no, thanks. I've a bike. I must stay to – to . . . ' Siren silenced, the ambulance bumped up the lane. Brewster stood up to wave at it. Two men got out and came smartly up the field, carrying a folding stretcher. 'Heart,' Mary heard

110

Brewster explaining as the men came near, then he glanced at the hovering couple and their cowed dog. It must have been an eloquent look for they turned to go.

After a quick exploratory feel of Ellis's heart pulse the ambulance crew placed him on the stretcher, then carried him carefully to their waiting vehicle. Mary, unable to move, saw Ellis's white face lift through the gate, disappear behind the hedge, then lift high again into the back of the ambulance. Siren wailing, it backed out of the lane, set off through *Tremawrth*. Brewster and Jones followed in their blue Sierra. Shortly afterwards the Landrover lurched out of the lane, Madeleine's arm waving to Mary who stood alone in the field. Oh God, she thought agonisedly, the whole thing's a messier mess now. Poor Ellis Bryn! He'd looked mortally ill. What can I say to the members? What does that matter now! Drained by the events and her previous anger Mary turned to depression.

Her eyes wandered over the melancholy landscape, the unobtrusive, small stacks of bricks, planks, tucked into the hedge-bottom down below. That builder wasted no time. He was definitely in it as well. Her shoulders slumped, Mary walked downhill to the bike beneath the dripping hazel. By the gate she turned to look back towards the drenched circles, hidden in the swirling rain. She could not have seen the earth trembling in one spot, then small, reddish cascades of it mound slowly near the first circle's centre, nor the black, huddled crow in nearby thorns, cocking a curious eye at the moving ground.

Now Alone

A short story by Jane Edwards
Translated by Elin Williams

The first thing that strikes you after all the busyness and the coming and going is silence. A strange and terrible silence. Silence as is in films after the music that accompanies horrors or villainy stops. A threatening silence. A silence that amplifies every little noise into a loud bang: the sudden creak in the wall, the crack in the television, the screech of the telephone. Unexpected noises. You're on tenter-hooks. This silence is taking its toll on you.

Yours had always been a quiet house. You hated noise. That is why you never socialised much. Never joined societies and organizations; never went visiting or kept an open door; were never a member of a church or a party. An agoraphobic, according to the questionnaire that you had read in a women's magazine. The first step to overcoming agoraphobia is admitting your illness publicly. Taking part in a radio programme perhaps, and be labelled a hypochondriac in the bargain! How convenient it is to label things! Living seems so much easier! Schizophrenic, paranoiac, neurotic, alcoholic, illegitimate, nag, bachelor, widow.

Widow.

A sinister, ugly word You don't want to hear it. A black, dark word. *Keep away* is written under it in small print. Switch on the radio. The noise is too loud, too raucous for an empty house. Turn the volume down. Harsh alien voices fill your house, permeating every corner. Men and women harbingers of doom.

A killing in Belfast . . . a suicide in Wales . . . imprisonment worldwide . . . crimes in America . . . war in the Middle East . . . famine in Ethiopia . . . children suffering . . . a shortage of coal, gas, electricity, oil: a state of emergency.

Everything happening. Everything that is sad and terrifying. But nothing as sad as what happened to you: nothing that could compare to your bereavement. Not one loss as great.

Missing company, and that missing turning life inside out. No routine to meals. No meals to plan. '*A shame that you don't have any children,*' said some who called. A *lifeboat*. A pity that I didn't have a lifeboat to take me far, far away to some Utopia.

A small medicinal drop of whisky would do you good, except that the doctor had warned you to be careful while still taking the tablets. Tablets to raise your spirits. Better not mix them with drink or it will be the end of you. In giving you these tablets the doctor put a terrifying choice in your hands. The choice makes you light-headed, disturbing the butterflies in your stomach. The choice moves before your eyes like a rope hanging from the ceiling: like the pendulum of a clock. The choice is simple. Life never was full to the brim of happiness and sunshine. And yet, there was order, and you prided yourself in that order. Washing day. Ironing day. Baking day. Meals on time. Meals to plan. Routine.

Being without routine is like climbing stairs that have no banisters.

Being without routine is like swimming in a whirlpool.

Being without routine is like being shut in a dark room.

Every night at five before it gets dark you lock the doors, and then make sure that they are locked before going to bed. This is the new routine – perhaps.

The morning is the saddest part of the day, the afternoon the longest and the night the worst. What or who decides when it is bedtime? Just not getting used to the fact that there's no one to turn to for a chat. One night when you were about to go to bed the phone rang. And ever since you've waited for the same thing to happen again. That night you slept like a log. You will the same thing to happen again. It's strange how life is sustained on a sprig of longing.

Sometimes people call. The faithful ones. All women. Each time someone came to the door you felt like running anywhere to hide, and each time they prepared to go you searched for every excuse to keep them in your front room. You had an intense interest in their family life. You were forever searching through your cupboards for food or some piece of clothing to give them. No one goes home empty-handed.

You're a prey for spinsters. They close in upon you like spiders. They are longing to make you one of them. A ring is an asset. A ring that's yellow like honey. When these get their hands on you, you cease to be a person. Perhaps it's a number you have: 38. Why 38? Because that's how old you are – perhaps. There is no club for spinsters.

One of the women, who's younger than you, is eager to come to live with you. She's fat and has skin that perspires grease. She wears powder as if she's been raised in a circus. And the perfume. Oh! How you hate her perfume. She's full of fuss tidying the papers, plumping up the cushions and making cups of tea. Her fat hands touch everything, longing to touch every material; dish; paper; bit of clothing; flesh.

She is the one who succeeds in bringing you out of your cocoon of self pity where you've been dawdling so long. She and her fat hands and her compulsion to touch everything. You despise her and her compulsion, and regard it with disgust, like long ago when you were innocent and beginning to sense what went on between a man and a woman. Remembering the noises from your parents' bedroom; remembering seeing two on top of each other in a field; remembering Dei with his trousers down

114

to his knees trying to tempt you into his house. You running for your life and promising yourself a life of purity in a convent. A convent where flesh is hidden under a black habit. A convent where everyone is clean and pure under her black habit thinking pure beautiful thoughts.

The fat powdered one must be kept out of your house. But there's no moving her. It is as if she knows that you are crouched behind the sofa or hiding under the bed. Never in bed. Never in bed. You could not bear to let her dream about you lying in bed. You must go out to avoid her.

You keep away from restaurants and sea-sides and places that seem to be reserved especially for families. The sound of people saddens you. You feel sorry for yourself.

Then one night, in a dream, someone nameless, faceless climbs into your bed. He touches you. You didn't want him to touch you. But the touch gives pleasure although it never reaches a climax. The feeling stays with you all day: that ache between your legs, the itching longing. You make yourself work to try to forget, but it still burns. You know of a way to dull it. But that is not enough. That never was enough. Your sights and dreams turn to men.

Little had you realised when bereavement came your way that this would come so soon. So shamefully soon.

But others had realised. Men who seemed respectable. Some who worked with your husband and knew him well. What is it that's given you away? The shine in your eyes? Your walk? Your smile?

Their lust is repulsive: the look in their eyes that says *you're ready for me . . . ready for a man*. The heat between your legs freezes as they look at you with their greedy eyes. You make a big thing of asking them about their wives and children. You buy a long high-necked, long-sleeved black dress to hide your flesh.

You put your fancy on a boy with long curly hair who works in next door's garden every Saturday afternoon. He's a heavy smoker and sounds as if he suffers from whooping cough. You've never seen anyone as pale as him. Whenever you are around he sings Welsh melodies and hymns. He has a tenor voice. You haven't spoken to him – yet. You have a great interest in gardening every Saturday afternoon. Your dreams and fantasies concentrate solely on the gardener.

He's reticent to talk to you. He lets his actions speak on his behalf. One Saturday afternoon he cut a thick branch from an ash tree with his bare hands and hurled it at your feet.

But you do not have the patience to play games. One Saturday afternoon you decide to pull up the gooseberry bush by its roots. You struggled for a long time. But at last the device works and the boy jumps over the hedge into your garden.

He pulls up the bush in no time. He's so able although he has a nasty cold. You advise him to go to see a doctor, but he sees too many of them already. He's in and out of hospitals: a shadow on his lung – or a growth. Nobody's quite sure. The smoking does him no good but he wouldn't thank anyone for having to live without a smoke. He works in a factory making saucepans and frying pans. A factory isn't a very healthy place for someone with a lung complaint. You invite him into the house for a cup of tea. He's not comfortable in the house. The doctors have warned him that he must have plenty of fresh air. You open the windows so wide that the draught raises the curtains and threatens to knock the Dresden from the mantelpiece. He complains that the sun's in his eyes. His eyes are watering. You doubt whether he'll live long. You see the writing on the wall. You invite him for a cup of tea the following Saturday. His name is Gomer. A good, strong name. A name fit for a minister's son.

You can't wait much longer, his cold's getting worse: he's deteriorating. He's so pale, so thin, especially his long legs, his long thin bent legs. Seeing him look so unwell, you lose your head and invite him to see the bedrooms. You're behaving impulsively, exactly as if death itself is at the door. But he doesn't want to see the bedrooms. He's retreating. He has retreating eyes.

'Come on,' you say in your most authoritative voice, determined to show him your beautiful double bed, the double bed with the pink flowery quilt.

He has a nasty bout of coughing until he's doubled up. You manage to persuade him to rest under the pink quilt in his working shoes. You take out a snowy white handkerchief from the drawer to dry the sweat from his brow. The handkerchief smells of fresh lavender. He's smiling.

It was you who bent your head to kiss him first. You would like to think that it happened the other way around. But looking back in cold blood, you know that it was you who started the whole business. His lips were warm and tasted of tobacco. His lips were warm wet and sent shivers through your body. There weren't enough tobacco-tasting kisses made for you. You draw your fingers through his dusty hair and pull him closer. His body hardens and tightens.

Man in all his glory is the most magnificent thing ever created.

He gets up from the bed to take off his clothes. You follow him. But he's shy, he doesn't want you to see him naked. He turns his back on you and crouches. He hides his underwear under the bed in case you see how grey they are. His body is like a bow, thin as a reed. He glances at you shyly and turns his head away. Some of his discomfort rubs off on you and you pull the bedclothes up to your chin. Your teeth are chattering. Not from cold. No, not from cold.

For a minute you're thinking of women all over the world who have lived without this. Without passion. Without desire. Without longing. Without burning.

When he enters the bed you are both shy and afraid of touching, exactly as you're afraid of the first touch of cold waves in the sea. He looks at you with surprised confusion before rushing to embrace you and hide his shyness in your hair. He stays like that for a while until he warms. He doesn't have a wrinkle on his pale face. It is obvious that he's very young and inexperienced. You open your thighs to contain him fully. You draw him into the circle of your experience.

His body tightens and his breathing comes faster. He blows in your ears and plays with your breasts as if they were sponges. His tobacco-tasting kisses are wet all over your face. He hurls himself upon you.

NO. NO. NO . . . O . . . O . . . NO.

You push him off roughly and give him a very small package from under the pillow. He gazes in surprise at the package in his hand, as if he's never seen one before. Hardly! You tell him to put it on. He has to put it on. You don't want to conceive.

Farewell respectability! You have just pushed the secret of your life into his hands; a small yellow piece like silk. You'd better wear it, mate.

You're like a block of ice, like driftwood. But he is sleeping. In a while he'll wake up and mumble something about going, without looking at you, of course. God's speed! God, God's speed!

You are crying – it's your inside that's crying. You are crying for the pure days of your childhood. You remember being in front of the fire counting the buttons on your liberty bodice. Twenty-four. That made you Queen. You remember your grandmother reaching for the baked potatoes from the embers in the grate. You remember making a mouse with your handkerchief in chapel when it was winter and everyone was as warm as toast and redeemed. You remember your mother letting everyone give the Christmas pudding a stir in the earthenware bowl on the kitchen table. You remember lying in a tubful of cold water in the sun. You remember lying in your bed dreaming of being a nun.

You don't want to remember the gardener and the small package under the pillow. You would give anything to forget the gardener and the contempt in his eyes as he left you.

You didn't see him after that. He didn't come back to work

in next door's garden. Perhaps he died from a lung disease. Perhaps he emigrated to Australia where there's plenty of fresh air and sun – perhaps. Perhaps he escaped from you. Perhaps.

There's no point in going on. Everyone who's lost a dear one knows of the troubles that follow: the misery and the grief; the loss and the loneliness; the tortures of the flesh. Experiences for which you have not been prepared. Confusing, degrading experiences often. And one bereavement seeming to give birth to another each time. But however unpleasant the experiences were – a fat, powdered woman pushing herself into your house, a young inexperienced boy escaping from your bed, – they were means to support you. Salvation came from unlikely places.

* * *

It is a fact known to many by now that the author of the above is Hannah Rhydderch. It was broadcast on the popular radio programme, *Merched yn Bennaf*, and later published in *Y Cymro* and *Barn*. Before long it was translated into English for the expensive *Nova* magazine, and it was broadcast on Woman's *Hour*.

The piece became famous as a result of the astonishing reaction it generated. Through the BBC, the papers and the magazines mentioned, the author received a torrent of letters, letters from Wales mostly, but some came from as far as New Zealand and Hong Kong.

What accounted for its appeal? After all, a great many confessions which are just as personal can be read in magazines every week; in fact, washing dirty linen in public is extremely popular in our age. And we are quite used to hearing the complaints of homosexuals and lesbians.

Hannah Rhydderch's confession was different. It was written not by a member of an organisation or a particular group, but by an individual in her distress. The confession was like a desolate cry from the heart, a cry by a young woman voicing her deepest experiences publicly. It was her honesty that appealed to people, and her open manner of discussing this problem which is at the same time a hidden problem and a problem that is common to thousands of widowed mature women.

To us who have not faced the excrutiating experience of losing a partner, Hannah Rhydderch's confession, when we first heard it, was an eye-opener. Whenever we heard of someone losing a partner we thought in terms of loss and grief, thinking in the abstract, we could almost say spiritually, without considering the needs of the flesh. In an age that has made the flesh such a public thing, it is strange that the passion and desires of normal women who have been left lonely have not been discussed more.

Doesn't your society expect widowed men and women to lead a pure blameless life? And do we not tut-tut and shake our heads when we hear of someone dating before the body of her husband is cold in his grave? Passion does not have a timetable nor desire its specified period. It is a need, a craving that must be satisfied. But society in its prejudice condemns that need when it comes to some of its members.

This is how it should be, we say. Reality is different, said Hannah Rhydderch, going on brazenly to describe her experiences. That was like opening a floodgate. A torrent of widowed women rushed to write to her pouring out their confessions without so much as hiding behind a false name or anything. For them, writing was an act of faith, an act of trust, a step in the dark fully believing that there were friendly arms there to support them.

And who could blame them? Had not this brave woman, by describing her own pitiful state, given their woes a layer of respectability by bringing them out into the daylight? Who better to write to, and what simpler way to purge the conscience?

Some months after the broadcast and the publishing, everyone who had written to Miss Rhydderch received a note from her thanking them for writing, and telling them that they could read more on the subject when she published her book in the near future.

True enough. A year and a half later the book appeared under the title *Ar Golli Cymar:* a collection of letters and a praiseworthy effort to categorise, interpret and define them. About the same time, the English version of the book was published, *Now Alone.* In order to promote sales the author went on a tour of America to discuss the book on television and with various societies.

But strangely, she did not appear on television in Wales or England, and no picture of Hannah Rhydderch was seen in any paper or magazine. It is the letters that account for the sweeping success of the book – over four thousand copies were sold of the Welsh version and about forty thousand of the English – namely the letters the author received after her famous confession.

Yes, every single correspondent was betrayed by her. Their confessions were published without consent. And that is why so many hundreds of women all over the world hate the name of Hannah Rhydderch, and fear that people will recognise them in the book.

But who is Hannah Rhydderch? Where does she come from? What is her background? Why is there not a picture of her available? Why are the BBC and the publishers of the magazines so unwilling to divulge any information about her?

I have for some time been seeking answers to my questions. And have wandered down many tracks before finding Miss Rhydderch, not so far from my own home here in Gwynedd. Hannah Rhydderch, or Lisa Parry, as she now calls herself, is a tall shapely woman with long curly red hair down to her waist. But, doubtless, before this article sees the light of day she will have changed her name again and moved. She refused to let me photograph her.

She was unwilling to divulge much about herself, but after pressing her I was told this much: she was born in Bangor some twenty-seven years ago, the daughter of a shop-keeper. After graduating in Music at Manchester University she taught for a while in Liverpool. As she did not enjoy the work she left and went to work on the buses; after this she worked in a café and as a *lady's companion* to a widow.

That was when the idea of writing the radio piece came to her.

Those who were deceived by her were totally blind, she said.

She is unmarried, and obviously quite able to fend for herself. It is insecure people, she said, who marry, weak people who are looking for a refuge outside themselves.

She is now collecting material for her next volume. *Llosgach yng Nghefn Gwlad (Incest in Rural Wales)*. People of Gwynedd, beware of her smiles and do not encourage her on any account. She is dangerous.

If you have reason to doubt me, then read her confession again, and read it very very carefully, noticing how falsely it was written by this ambitious woman from Bangor.

Foxy

Glenda Beagan

Into the cornfields of the Philistines the burning foxes run.
Red gold of the foxes. Red of the flames. Gold of the corn.

I've decided to be me. I know it's living dangerously but I've made up my mind. This is me as I really am. All the highs and all the lows. Intact.

And almost immediately the dreams start. Ordinary daytime things become extraordinary night time marvels. Fine. So far. It's when the extravaganza of sleep slips over into the hours of daylight that the trouble starts. This time though, when the storm comes, I intend to ride it.

I'm an artist. Well, I used to be an artist. But the marvels became terrors and my well-meaning husband Giles persuaded me to get expert help. Those were the words he used. Dr Drysdale's expert help was very expensive but his prescriptions worked well. I had no complaints. For peace of mind I was prepared to jettison every creative atom in me. I was thankful for the calm.

And then I met Foxy.

I'm jumping ahead of myself. I must tell you how I came to this outpost in the mountains, this cottage at the end of a narrow valley in north Wales. Our home is called Cae Llwynog. Foxfield in English, but it sounds so ordinary in English. And there's

123

nothing ordinary about this place. Its signature is slate. Look one way and you see nothing but the old quarry workings, the great heaps of slate waste that are almost mountains in themselves. It has its own kind of beauty. Its light and shade, its cloudscapes. I never knew there were so many shades of grey.

I didn't want to come here at all. We had our rural retreat in the Rodings, so easy to get to and from London, so charming too. We still own it, but for the most part Giles rents it out to friends. And friends of friends. But why Wales, I said, nearly seven years ago when he bombarded me with estate agents' brochures and I met Foxy. Well, it was her cub I met initially. He stepped out of the bracken like a little ginger puppy. I nearly fell over him! And he held up his paw as if he wanted me to shake hands with him. You know sometimes things *are* just too cute to be true. Ghastly word cute, I know, but there you are.

The fox cub was there for just a moment and then he seemed to dematerialise back into the bracken. I scanned the bare grassy part of the hillside beyond and sure enough a little while later they emerged, a vixen and three cubs. She stopped and stared at me, at a safe distance, admittedly, but quite without concern.

And that was my first encounter with Foxy.

As I said, I'm an artist. And what I'd hoped would happen happened. Even before I'd stopped the tablets completely the dreams came back. And the ideas, weird ideas sometimes, but I welcomed them all. Not that my first drawings were in the least bit weird.

One of the things you can't help noticing when you come to Wales is the chapels because even the smallest village has at least two of them. I reckon there must've been terrific competition between all the denominations, Baptists and Wesleyans and Calvinists and Congregationalists, all of them striving to build the grandest and the best. Not terribly Christian that, perhaps, and now as the increasingly elderly worshippers decline and die the chapels do the same. More and more you see these often huge places standing empty.

The quintessentially Welsh scene for me is one of an ornately pillared and porticoed chapel set behind railings and wrought iron gates, with, in the background, a hint of mist and fir trees. And then there are those heaps of broken slate glinting in the rain.

Anyway, I started to draw chapels.

I went looking for them. Since I lost my nerve with driving I've taken to the buses in a big way, bizarrely irregular and infrequent as they may be. My chapel studies started as strict architectural drawings. It was as if I had to re-educate my eye. And hand. There'd been a time when I could execute the finest precision drawings with ease. Not now. It was painstakingly hard work. Then, as I grew more confident, I started to sketch more loosely, more in my original style. It was as if I'd had to get back to the mechanics of drawing itself and be sure of that before I could allow myself a freer rein. When Giles came up one weekend after I'd managed to produce quite a fortfolio, I showed him them and was pleased for two reasons, first that he liked them and was glad that I'd revived my former skills, and secondly, and most importantly, that he still had no idea that I'd stopped the medication. There was no real reason why he should have guessed it, since I was perfectly relaxed and contented, but in a way it did indicate how little he understood me. He didn't seem to make the connection. It didn't occur to him that it was strange I should suddenly take up my art again, after years of not even thinking about it.

Cae Llwynog stands on its own at the end of the valley facing the village in an oblique sort of way, looking out on the hugest, grandest chapel you ever saw. Engedi. It was the first chapel I drew, naturally, as it was right on my doorstep. It's been closed for some years now. The few remaining members of the congregation must have rattled about in its vastness, and running costs must have been punitive. I'm not surprised it had to close its doors for the last time and perhaps there's a moral to the story after all. Of the three chapels in the village, this, the biggest and the most grandiose, was the first to close, whilst the smallest and most modest of the three, the plain whitewashed Gosen, is now the only one in use.

Engedi is still an extraordinary monument, its façade being so over the top ornamental it takes some getting used to. Frankly, it's ugly, but so confident in its ugliness as to be almost endearing. I tried to imagine how the original worshippers must have saved and saved to build it, how they must have pondered over the builders' style books of the day before deciding on this dubious combination of Classical pillars and Gothic stained glass in windows incongruously like portholes, except for one quasi rose window dominating all. The whole thing looks sad now. It's emblazoned with FOR SALE signs, and more recently, and more desperately, MAY LET signs as well.

There was never a dull moment at Cae Llwynog. I augmented my chapel sketches with landscapes, moody monochrome things that wouldn't please the tourist but reflected the mountains more truly than sky blue prettiness and sunshine. And I took an increasing interest in the wild life of the area, sketching that too, especially the birds, kestrels and buzzards and the wonderful ravens, nesting high up on the quarry terraces. They're so talkative, constantly chattering amongst themselves. In spring and way into our brief summer, I would listen out for them calling to each other as they soared. And how utterly different were these calls from the harsh croaks we commonly associate with ravens. They were notes of joy, clear as bells.

And all the time I was getting to know Foxy. If a day came and went without my catching at least a glimpse of her I felt quite bereft. I would often go walking up in the hills behind Cae Llwynog, looking for her in a way, I suppose, though at first it hadn't seemed that straightforward. I had only recently acquired this confidence, to go walking on my own. To make me feel really safe though, I always took my grandfather's walking stick along with me, my talisman. It had been kept all these years as a thing of beauty rather than for its practical application, but practical it most certainly was nonetheless and I loved its smooth dark wood, its shape, its fine sense of balance and the band of enscrolled silver on it. I reckoned it brought me luck.

I'd been reading about Australian aboriginal art in one of the journals I'd started subscribing to again. The article was a bit of a hybrid, part artistic critique, part anthropology, but I was fascinated by what it said about the way those truly native people acquire their totems. They don't choose their totems. Their totems chose them. Surely Foxy had chosen me. I found this whole idea thrilling. I watched her and her little family with growing fascination. I found places where it was easy simply to sit and wait for her to come by. I never tried to hide from her at all. I got to know her body language, what I can only describe as her gestures, her means of communication and believe me, she did communicate. She was not in the least afraid of me and though I never tried to get too close to her and her cubs, I knew that on some level she accepted me. I was not an outsider, not to her. One evening I remember in particular, one of our special September sunsets turning the mountains into a paintbox. I sat there quietly watching Foxy at the edge of the woods. We were both perfectly still, looking sort of sideways at each other. Then as the lightshow moved slowly across the sky the glory of it caught her magnificent white bib and turned it pink, no, more a deep cochineal. She was thin, crumpled and shabby after all that breeding and nurturing, but still with her rich brick colour. Now she was regal. Just sumptuous. And still we watched each other. A mutual frank approval. I felt I accessed her pure intelligence.

I was conscious though, and, not for the first time, that despite the proximity and acceptance of my totem, I could never be a true native. Love of a place is not enough. But even if my ancestry and my language debarred me from really belonging in human terms perhaps I could be redeemed by knowledge. I determined to get to know this land and the creatures of this land in the deepest way possible. It was not going to be just a matter of enjoyable country walks any more. It would involve a proper thorough-going study. I would keep a nature journal. I would observe more rigorously, not simply to enjoy the sights and sounds around me but to understand their interaction, their constant interplay. I would become a true ecologist.

The next time Giles came up he seemed to be rather amused by my acquisition of binoculars and reference books and my new interest in his ordnance survey maps. I thought he was being patronising and told him so, my earnestness alerting him for the first time that there was, maybe, a difference in me. He began to look at me rather quizzically, keeping his thoughts to himself, though, because Adrian Wallender was staying with us. Giles had shown him my portfolio of chapel studies and he was most enthusiastic. Adrian knows what he's talking about so when he suggested I choose the best of them and write a little history of the chapels, explaining the relevance of each name, for instance, and then send them off to *Resonant Image*, I was all ears. And then he said something about the name Engedi, and how it struck him as strange.

It sounds really Welsh, he said. Don't you think?

And it suddenly struck me too. Yes, it did sound Welsh. It was also unusual. The Horebs and the Salems and the Seions might be commonplace but Engedi was different, special, and, as far as I knew, a one off. I had no idea what it referred to either, so next time I went on the bus to Caernarfon I found myself in the library poring over a Biblical Concordance. Here it was, in the Book of Samuel, the story of David and King Saul, their enmity, and Saul's spies informing him that David was hiding in 'the strongholds of Engedi'. I liked the ring of that, and how, while Saul slept in a mountain cave with all his men about him, David crept up from within the cave's depths and cut off a section of his garment, challenging him later by holding up the piece of cloth to prove how easily he might have killed the sleeping king. Why did this story appeal so much to our valley's quarrymen that they named their proud new chapel after it? I was none the wiser, unless they too thought the word had a Welsh sound to it, and liked, as I did, the idea of 'the strongholds'. For surely these mountains were still a language and a culture's strongholds, even today. I kept repeating the phrase to myself. It had an appropriately bleak, astringent music, did the strongholds of Engedi, with paradoxically, at the same time, a kind of friendliness.

As I sat there in the library the concordance flicked open to a nearby page and I saw the word 'fox'. Quite casually I looked up the reference in the Book of Judges and read on, intrigued by an astonishing story of lust and violence and horrible revenge. I read with horror and incredulity about Samson gathering together three hundred foxes (now quite how did he do that?) setting fire to their brushes (the implication being that he did this rather as a chainsmoker lights one cigarette from another) and then letting them run loose, the poor panicking things, into the Philistine fields. It was the time of the harvest.

Red gold of the foxes. Red of the flames. Gold of the corn.

I felt that this was my image, that these were my colours. I can't explain it. I was exhilarated, appalled too, but I have to say mostly exhilarated. Something rushed up and out in me, like a log-jam breaking. I knew with growing excitement and conviction that this would become a painting, by far the best, by far the strongest thing I'd ever done. The background of it was there in my mind immediately, familiar as breathing.

Here was my stronghold of Engedi. Here was the view from Cae Llwynog, the row of quarrymen's cottages with the circlet of hills behind, the stark geometrics of the quarry, the heaps of waste and then the chapel itself, handsome and new, a congregation descending its front steps following a sermon, a nineteenth century congregation dressed in all their Sunday finery. A woman is prominent amongst them. She stands a little apart, pointing out across the valley, the foreground of the painting. It was one expanse of wheat. And it's starting to burn, but you guessed that. The painting has a split personality, half painted entirely realistically and with meticulously detailed control, half executed as a Dionysian welter, violently surreal. Half is grey, dark, wet, sombre. You can see the fronds of fern amongst the stones, the individual bricks in the wall. You can smell wet bombazine, wet gaberdine and serge, and the wet leather of hymnbooks. Half is an inferno, of stalks and seedheads, smelling horribly of burning leaf and grain, of singeing hair and fur. And amongst the corn run the glorious flaming foxes, consumed by their own fire, the colours of the sun.

I bought my acrylics, my boards. And I couldn't wait to get home. Did I know then that my latest craziness had begun? I think maybe I did, but if I did, I know, too, that I embraced it.

Like a Duck to Water

Phil Carradice

I woke suddenly, bright sunlight streaming in through the canvas walls. Paul was already up, struggling to pull on his socks at the far end of the tiny tent.

'Morning,' he grinned. 'Better get a move on – some of the boys are already up.'

I snorted and rolled over in my sleeping bag.

'From the noise they made last night I'd have thought some of them never went to bed.'

'Put the kettle on, Dave,' called Paul.

I put my head out of the tent doorway and watched as big Dave moved over to the water container. He raked the embers of the previous evening's fire, dropped a few twigs onto the sparks and kindled the flame.

'Be about ten minutes,' he called.

'He's been a great kid this week,' I said, inclining my head towards Dave. 'Really taken to the hills.'

We crawled out of the tent and stood looking down at the lake which lay a few hundred yards away. In the fragile heat of early summer it shimmered like a million broken bottles. Give it a few hours, I thought, and the place would be full of canoeists and swimmers from the Outdoor Pursuits Centre further down

131

the valley. But for now it was still and untarnished – as it should be.

'Tea's ready,' called Dave and we moved across to the fire.

He poured out three mugs and we sat in silence, gazing at the lake. Behind us the Snowdon massif with its linking battlements of Crib Goch Ridge reared like a giant's knuckles against the empty sky.

Presently Dave picked up a twig and began to poke it idly at the fire.

'So what are we doing today?' he asked.

'Nothing much. We thought we'd treat it as a rest day. Walking the Snowdon Horseshoe yesterday really beat up some of the younger kids. We'll let them have a lie in, then after Brian arrives we'll probably go down to the beach for the afternoon.'

We had been in north Wales for just over a week. It had been a hectic time – rock climbing, hill walking and the occasional educational visit thrown in for good measure. As always when we were away from school the boys had been perfect, in particular big Dave.

Back at school he always seemed such a misfit, a bit of a gentle giant, too clumsy for comfort and with a large face too lined and angular for his age. But here, on the hills of Snowdonia, he had found his vocation. Dave took to the mountains like an Alpine guide. He seemed to have a real feel for the rocks and terrain and covered the miles with great efficiency and skill.

'What time's Brian due, then?' he asked suddenly.

'We don't really know,' said Paul. 'He finished his course yesterday and was planning to come straight down this morning. Could be any time.'

Dave sighed.

'He should have a letter for me, from Jane. She said she'd write last week but we left before the post arrived.'

'Are you still going up to Manchester to see her next week?'

Dave grinned and nodded.

'If I get enough money. I've saved my pocket money for the last few weeks but I'm still a few quid short.'

'Don't go bunking the train,' I said, 'or you'll be in trouble with the law again. You know what the magistrate said. Any more problems and they'll send you away – Youth Custody or Borstal this time.'

Dave grunted but said nothing.

'You can clean my boots if you like,' Paul commented, raking up the fire to brew more tea. 'I'll give you fifty pence for it.'

He was joking but Dave was more than willing to do anything that would help him find the money he needed. A quick scout around all the staff for jobs produced only a pound. Then Dave had an idea.

'Tell you what. I'll bet you all a pound each that I could run up that hill without stopping.'

He pointed at the high ridge that overlooked us. From where we sat it must have been eight hundred feet to the top, maybe even a thousand, and although it was covered in grass the sides of the slope were exceptionally steep. We had walked it on our first day and the effort had left us all breathless and winded.

'Don't be bloody silly,' said Paul. 'You'd never do it.'

'Of course I could,' retorted Dave. 'Come on, a pound each. I'll run it, no trouble.'

We talked it over and decided he would be lucky to reach half way. Dave had never been particularly strong on sticking to his guns; we knew he would give up before he hurt himself. And if, by some miracle, he did manage it then the poor devil could do with the money.

'OK,' I said, 'but if you stop just once then the deal's off.'

He grinned and disappeared into his tent. By now the other boys and staff had appeared and sat happily alongside us by the fire, waiting for their unexpected treat. In a few moments Dave was back, dressed in gym shorts and rugby jersey.

'See you later,' he said and began to run down the track that led to the floor of the valley.

'He'll never make it,' said someone. 'And what if he hurt himself?'

Nobody answered. We sat watching his progress. Presently he reached the foot of the ridge, turned to wave and started up the slope.

Slowly, inch by inch, Dave moved upwards. He had learned his hill craft well. In wide zigzag arcs he traversed the ridge, moving back and forth across our fields of vision. Across and across he went but always upwards, ever upwards. Paul fetched his binoculars and trained them on the jogging boy.

'He's having a bloody good go at it.'

We watched, each of us trying to imagine the searing agony of breath as it rasped up in his chest; the bone shuddering jolt of his feet as they slapped like wet fish, up and down upon the hill. It didn't take the greatest intellect in the world to work out he must be going through hell up on the side of that ridge.

'Rather him than me,' said Paul, slowly shaking his head.

Suddenly I heard a shout from the road below. A car had pulled to a halt at the beginning of the farm track and Brian, our newest member of staff, was coming rapidly up the hillside towards us. We waved and, shortly, he joined us.

'You're early,' drawled Paul. 'We didn't expect you till later this morning.'

We explained what was happening, why we were waiting with our eyes glued to the ridge. Brian sat with us to watch Dave's progress.

'I've got a letter for him in my bag,' he said. 'Manchester postmark.'

While we had spoken Dave had passed the halfway point. His movements were not so fluid, perhaps, and occasionally he missed his footing or stumbled in a hollow. His speed had slowed considerably and he was now going no faster than a brisk walk but there was no denying that each second took him closer to the top. A light breeze had sprung up – that, at least, would help to cool him. God knows, he would need it, I thought, he must be sweating blood up there.

'He's going to make it,' I said.

And he did. A few minutes later Dave stood, triumphant, on the top of the ridge. He sank to his knees and remained there for several long moments. At last, however, he straightened, turned to face us and waved once. Then, carefully, painfully, he began to come down.

'I'd never have believed it,' said Paul.

'Give him credit,' I said. 'He must be really desperate for that money.'

Paul sniffed.

'Desperate to see the girlfriend, anyway.'

When Dave finally arrived back he was exhausted. His breath came in shuddering great gasps while his legs buckled and shook as if they were made of rubber. He collapsed alongside the fire and for a long time lay with his eyes tightly shut. Finally, he sat up and grinned, eyes large and expectant in his elongated face.

'I did it,' he gasped. 'Pay up.'

We paid, dutifully. Then he saw Brian and smiled.

'Finally got here, did you? Any letters for me?'

Brian passed across a brown envelope.

'Sealed with a loving kiss, Dave,' he said.

We brewed tea while Dave read his letter. The other boys went off for their morning swim in the lake while we exchanged small talk with Brian. Then, suddenly, Paul touched my knee and motioned towards Dave.

He was sitting, staring across at the ridge he had just climbed. The letter had fallen from his hand and lay, useless, at his feet.

'What's the matter, Dave?' I asked.

He looked up, startled, and gazed across – not at me, not at any of us; through us, perhaps, but not at us. Tears began to well up on his lower lids.

'It's Jane. She's finished with me. Her dad says she can't see me any more.'

We sat in silence, watching his agony. None of us knew what to say, how to ease his hurt. A premonition of disaster, a strange feeling of fear and failure, had suddenly descended over the camp site.

Then, in one swift, decisive movement, Dave leapt to his feet and started down the slope towards the lake. Brian made to go after him.

'Leave him,' I said. 'He isn't going far.'

We watched as he walked unsteadily down the hill, strangely out of place in his shorts and rugby jersey. He stopped and sat at the waters edge, an empty, forlorn figure with the morning breeze whipping at his hair.

And the letter he had dropped began to flutter in the wind, its pages ruffled and finally tumbled away one by one. Like lost dreams they spiralled in the sky, outlined against the ridge.

The Cuckoo's Time is April and May

Robin Llywelyn
Translated by Meic Stephens

I sat down at the base of a large tree to watch the sunlight play
among the leaves and listen to the world. Quietude is difficult
to come by, difficult to find. I wonder whether the cuckoo found
it somewhere? Or is it still searching the old peaceful lanes of
Eifionydd or Meirionnydd? Or is it tasting the warm grapes
which ooze towards it through the cloud on the horizon?
Anyway, quietude is even rarer. A pity to waste it, I thought,
with no one to be seen in the vicinity and none wandering the
beach below me. Not a soul today throwing sticks for their dogs.
Yes, I was staring up through the leaves of the tree. And the sun
was trying to wink at me from under the cloud and my gaze
was through the branches towards the acres of sand. The sand
of a tidal beach is tidy, isn't it? No weeds growing on it, nor the
remain of castles sinking into it.

I never saw her coming through the wood on tip-toe. If it
comes to that, I didn't see her going, either. What state are you
in? she asked. I don't know, I'm sure, I replied. I put up my hand
to stop the sun blinding me through the branches. The walls are
the same, I said, and the same old moss is on their tops. That's
what you think, she said, with the yellow of primroses in her
hair and the blue of wild hyacinths in her eyes, but we didn't

hear the cuckoo this year, did we? Perhaps it will come again soon, I said. Or perhaps it sings a different song now. The lands it has to fly over are too much for it, I suppose. I don't know anything about heat, she said, I prefer the rain. Rain is inevitable somehow, although it is also pleasant having the sun to play on your cheeks. But what's weather to me? Storm, a fair spell, winter, summer, I don't know anything about them. Do you sometimes hear another voice whispering in your ear?

She was looking at me as if expecting a reply. What good does it do to ask? I said. Sometimes, she said, it does. Only when the voices resound in the branches and slip between the leaves. Did you see how I searched for you while you were staring far out over the empty estuary? I saw nothing, I said, except the world over there and then I closed my eyes for an instant and saw you here with me waiting for the tide as night comes down. Yes, she said, but it's only leaves that can open without being able to close. I opened my heart once, she said then, and although the wound healed . . .

She came towards me and her face was close to mine. I held his hand, she said, and wasn't expecting clay in the river-bed nor the twinkling stars. His hand was cold, she said, but his forehead was running with sweat. I wiped it with my sleeve but he got to his feet until his shadow filled the place and his breath dulled the light coming in through the panes of the window. How long have I been awake?, he said then. I didn't know you were asleep, I replied, from the doorway, because I knew now that I had to go. I don't know where he is now or what he's doing. I suppose he thinks of me, if only occasionally. I sometimes think of him. I remember once, on the bare hillside, he came over the rise and sat beside me like before except that he was shy as he put his arm around my shoulder and tenderly kissed me under my ear. We won't go up onto the hill today, he said, it's threatening to rain and the hill is higher than I remember it, too. Small things like that make me think he remembers.

It's not all milk and honey for anyone, is it? I said, seeing her grow pale. She too was now staring out across the bay and shadows were moving across her eyes like clouds. Perhaps it wasn't with me she was talking. Only staring out and her lips moving. I never offered him anything, she said, only my heart. I still try to remember what my part in the bargain was supposed to be. And in the end I did get my heart back, though the worse for wear. The wound's healed now and the scar is very small. It's small and white here under my breast.

And when she lifted up her shirt there was the small white scar under her left breast. Love hurts dreadfully, I said, and yet we still crave it. Yes, I know, she said, rearranging her shirt. You're dreadful, too, for saying things that are obvious to everyone. They are easier to say than saying vague things, I said. It's easier to love than not to love, she said. Yes, I said, trying to think of something similar. It is easier to break than to uproot, I said then. It is easy to dirty fine white silk, she said. Faults are large where there is no love, she added. Great the hatred, and the love, she said again. Please, can we not talk in allegories all the time? I said. It is easy for the healthy who have no pain to urge the infirm to take solace, she said. Yes, I know that, I said, trying to recall my proverbs. Sufficient unto the day is the pudding thereof, I said. Enough of crowder and harp, I added. Enough is enough of singing the same song, enough is enough of honey on the fire. Enough is a little more than what you have, and enough pudding will choke six dogs. And then I shut up.

She was sitting at the base of the green tree and watching me intently. Every bird enjoys its own song, she said, starting to undo her shirt again. I didn't know any proverbs for things like that. It's pleasant to wear two shirts, she said sternly as she slipped the fine white silk from her shoulders. And here is skin without any shirt! And then she whirled the garment about her and flung it away over the gorse and I saw her angrily bare-breasted before me and her eyes were flashing lightning and her

139

hands on her hips. She threw back her head, lifting her hair to the breeze. Wear it, then, she said, wear it over your shirt. Let me see you, in your two shirts. And she pointed at the gorse-bush with its thorns pricking the light silk, and the moon was rising over the rim of the mountain.

I held the shirt between finger and thumb and its perfume was of May flowers and I drew it through my fingers and wrapped it round me like a white flag, like the sail of a sunlit boat on Aber Henfelyn and the breeze in the flowers of the gorse was yellow and the silk fell around me like foaming waves. For such a petite one she likes her shirts large, I thought. This isn't a blouse of a shirt, I said to myself, but a Bendigeidfran's cloak of a shirt, the rough apron of the Anglesey giantess, a parachute of a shirt, by jiminy. You must be a sort of goddess, I said, having managed to get my head out between two buttons, only goddesses could wear a shirt as noble as this.

The moonlight was bathing her skin and the sound of the tide filling the beach. The next thing I knew she was pulling off her skirt. I was still struggling with the silk shirt. Take it off, she said. What? I said. Why? Because it's high tide and a full moon, she replied. Come on, we'll go for a bathe. I don't like bathing in the sea, I said, and the gorse needles are thick underfoot and it would be best if we started thinking of going home. And who said I'd come with you? she said, kicking her skirt away and starting to step gingerly over the gorse needles towards the sea-rocks. Come on, she said, the water isn't cold . . . well, not very. By the time I had climbed down to the rocks she had swum half-way to the island; I could see her bobbing like a white cork in the middle of the bay as I dipped my toes into the water. I'm coming, I said, trying to shout but the breeze was against me. And the water was cold.

I didn't catch up with her, no, I had no hope of overtaking her with her swimming like a white eel. Perhaps she's a mermaid, I thought, but then they don't have any legs. She was waiting for me on the rocks of the island. Come on, she said, hurry up. Where are we going? You'll see. The sea-water ran like pearls down her back and her hair hung in coils over one shoulder. I saw her white hand being raised and her fingers beckoning. We joined hands and they were cold. Some Englishman's bought the island, she said, and he has a smashing holiday home over there. And that was where we went – she knew how to get in – and wrapped ourselves in blankets and lit a fire. This Holiday Home Englishman has some fine whisky, I said as we lay on a sheepskin in front of the fire, with crystal glasses tinkling like stars in our hands. It's only in this kingdom that we live like this, she said. What kingdom's that? I asked. No-man's kingdom, she replied. The old faraway look was back in her eyes. Yes, she said. Where we recognize without touching and get without seeking but seek nothing that's not already got. She glanced at me, adding, Do you recognize me? Yes, I said. You didn't, she said. Will I again? I asked. There's no next time in no-man's kingdom, she said. Why? I asked. Because there's no yesterday and no tomorrow, no watch and no grandfather clock. How do they know what time it is, then? I asked. Be quiet, she said. Only in no-man's kingdom are we allowed to live like that. But you won't gain it by searching, remember. And don't let your hand fail you when your turn comes to try and catch it, or you won't ever see it again. I see, I said, not fully understanding. So are you happy? Yes, she said. But why, I asked, if nothing lasts? Everything lasts for ever in no-man's kingdom, she said. But it was you who said it doesn't last, I said. The fire was dying in the grate and the dawn was grey at the window. I got to my feet and my shadow filled the floor and I wiped my breath from the window-pane to see the blue light of morning.

We could walk back along the beach, she said. The tide must be out by now. Yes, I said, looking across the dark sands.

I wonder whether that Holiday Home Englishman missed the two blankets; he probably did the whisky. Our feet were squelching in the sand and there were whisps of wild cloud in

141

the distant east. Strips of pools lay like oil where the sea had been . Seabirds calling. And part of the night lingered in the woods of the estuary and the dawn-chorus of small birds drowned the scream of the lonely seagulls out on the beach. My feet were tender after the sands, making me hop on one leg when the gorse-needles pricked my feet. She walked over the gorse needles without stumbling and grabbed her shirt from the bush. The morning light slunk towards us from every direction. She put on her shirt and it fitted her. I pulled on my trousers and did up my fly. I wiped my lips with the palm of my hand to taste the salt. She went over to her skirt which lay like a wreath on the ground and picked it up and shook it free of creepy things and leaves. The dew had soaked our clothes. She shivered as she drew the skirt over her ankles and up her legs. I was struggling to shove my feet into shoes that had just become two sizes too small for me. The din of the birds was filling the wood and ringing in my head. And she combed her hair with her fingers and brushed it back. And with the palm of her hand she caught a chink of the morning sunshine percolating through the branches onto her and held it as if it were a mirror in her hand. She turned to me and smiled. I caught the scent of bluebells and the smell of the beach. The light in the mirror of her hand was bright, and shining from her primrose hair and blue eyes. Slowly she turned her palm towards me and the light sparkled over me and filled me with its blessed warmth. I put my hand to my face and saw the hand light up as if a flashlamp were shining on it. I put my hand out to steady myself against the trunk of an oak-tree at my side. I could see the light borrowing into the recesses of the bark and disturbing insects and sending them scuttling to new hiding-places in their fright. No more than they could I look into the eye of the sun. And she was laughing through a cloud at the beginning of summer. I didn't see her go. I thought she was still there and that I should turn to her and laugh with her and talk about what we had seen. Then I thought I should see her when the cloud lifted from the face of the sun. But instead, raindrops began to fall on the leaves. Somewhere in the wood pigeons could be heard imitating the voice of the cuckoo. The cuckoo didn't call again this year. It wanted quietude, probably. I wonder whether it found it?

The Wonder at Seal Cave

John Sam Jones

Gethin stacked the returned books and wondered why Mr Bateman always seemed to do his marking in the middle study bay; why not the staff room, the small 'prep' room at the back of the biology lab, or even one of the other bays? Quite often, when he was putting books back in the geography section, nearest the study area, they'd smile at one another. Sometimes, if there was no one else in the library, they'd talk – but only if Mr Bateman initiated the conversation. Gethin liked these talks; he liked it that Mr Bateman seemed interested in what he was reading and what films he'd seen, or what he thought about mad cows, adulterous royals, and the war in Chechnya. Sometimes they even talked about football. When Gethin turned up for his library duty he found himself hoping that he and Mr Bateman would be alone, that there would be plenty of geography books to shelve, and that they might talk.

Mr Bateman was his favourite teacher; he was most people's favourite really. He got angry sometimes and shouted a bit, but he was never sarcastic, which seemed to be the weapon most of the male staff used to intimidate their classes into some kind of order and control. And he always made biology interesting, even if there were lots of facts that had to be memorised. He was the kind of teacher most students wanted to do well for, to please. The exam results pleased everyone; there were more A grades in biology from Ysgol yr Aber than from any other school in Wales and the school's record of success in biology was always used by the Welsh Office to challenge the cynicism of those opposed to Welsh-language science education.

Mr Bateman had learned to speak Welsh; perhaps this was what Gethin liked best about him. Very few of the English people who'd settled in the area had bothered to learn the language, but he had, and Gethin was hard put to detect an ill-formed mutation or a confused gender; Mr Bateman spoke better Welsh than many native speakers and Gethin admired him for the respect he'd shown to the language and culture of his adopted home. And there was football too; Gethin thought highly of him for that! Mr Bateman had grown up in Manchester and everyone at school knew how fanatically he still supported his home team – United, not City. Gethin supported Liverpool and went to some home games with Mel Tudor, Mel-siop-baco as everyone knew him, who had a season ticket at Anfield.

Gethin carried the Welsh novels back to their shelf wondering if he dared start a conversation with Mr Bateman. He needed to talk to somebody. The school summer holidays had been such a mixed time; although he'd been confident enough of good grades, waiting for the GCSE results had found him lurching between the certainty of staying on at school to do his A-levels and the uneasy emptiness of 'what if?'. It was then that 'the other thing' bothered him; it had been there for ages, of course, but 'doing well in your exams' and 'going to university like your brother and sister' had been a sufficient enough screen to hide behind. The kiss on *Brookside,* outing bishops and the debate about the age of consent had made the screen wobble a bit, but he really hadn't allowed himself to think very much that he might be, or what that might mean, until those moments of uneasy emptiness had folded over him. And now he knew that he was and he needed to talk about it.

He'd tried to talk to his sister. Gethin had stayed with Eilir in Liverpool at the beginning of July; he'd tried talking to her after seeing the film, but she'd seemed so taken up with her patients, her new boyfriend and the hassles she and her flat-mates were having with their landlord about the fungus growing on the kitchen wall. It was because she'd been so preoccupied that Gethin had spent his time in the city alone and had the chance to go to the cinema on a rainy afternoon. He'd read a review of *Beautiful Thing* in *The Guide* that came with Saturday's *Guardian*, and when he saw that it was showing at the ABC on Lime Street he'd loitered on the opposite pavement for almost an hour trying to muster up the courage to go in. It was the rain that eventually sent him through the glass doors into the garishly lit foyer of the cinema to face the spotty, many ear-ringed boy in the ticket booth who dispensed the ticket with a wry smile. Gethin had panicked, interpreting the boy's smile as 'I know you're queer . . . All the boys who come to see this film on their own are!' Only after taking his seat in the darkened auditorium did his panic subside.

It was a love story; Jamie and Ste, two boys his own age, falling in love with one another. There were no steamy love scenes and but for a fleeting glance at Ste's naked bottom there was no nudity, so Gethin got few clues as to what two boys might actually do together. When Jamie and Ste ran through the trees chasing one another and finally embracing and kissing, Gethin had become aroused; he'd wanted to be Jamie in the film – to be held and kissed by Ste . . . He'd wanted his own mother to be as accepting as Jamie's and he'd wanted a friend like Leah to talk to.

Outside the cinema it had stopped raining so Gethin decided to walk back to Eilir's flat near Princes Park. Wandering along Princes Avenue, he came to understand that something had changed in his life and nothing would be the same again. Behind the screen that he'd erected to keep himself from thinking about 'the other thing' he'd felt closed in silence – a silence which had left him anxious and uncertain, even fearful. But the screen had been pulled away by Jamie and Ste and their story had begun to give that unspeakable part of Gethin's life a shape. For the first time Gethin really understood what his father had so often preached to his congregation – 'that stories give shape to lives and that without stories we cannot understand ourselves'. Of course, the Reverend Llyr Jones had a certain anthology of stories in mind for giving shape to lives and Gethin knew that his father wouldn't include Jamie and Ste's story alongside those of Jacob, Jeremiah and Jesus. Llyr Jones wouldn't see the two boys' story as a 'beautiful thing'.

Gethin recalled that Sunday during the age of consent debate. His father, in a fiery sermon, had exhorted the congregation at Tabernacl (Methodistiaid Calfinaidd – 1881) to write to the local MP urging him to vote against lowering the age to sixteen. Gethin remembered the discussion over the roast beef after chapel, his father – with all the authority of an M.Th. and a dog-collar behind his words, saying that homosexuals were sinful and his mother – in her calm 'I'm the doctor, you can trust me' manner, saying that they were disturbed and needed psychiatric treatment.

Crossing Princes Park, Gethin sat by a reservoir of the city's debris that had once been a lake. He watched a used condom navigate its course on a stiffening breeze through the squalid waters between the half-submerged skeletons of an old bike and a supermarket trolley until it came to lie, stranded on the shore of an abandoned pram. He thought about his father and mother; how he loved them – but how he now didn't think he knew them at all. If he told them about the film – about Jamie and Ste and about what he now knew to be true of himself, would his father's love be acted out in some kind of exorcism and would his mother want the best medical care with visits to some psychologist? Gethin wondered if their love and trust in him were deep enough to challenge thirty years of belief in Calvinistic Biblical scholarship and 1960's medical science? A plastic baby's arm reached from the crib of slime in which it lay, grasping an empty sky; Gethin wondered if his reaching out would be as futile. Back at the flat, Eilir wanted to talk about her first AIDS patient – and about the fungus on the kitchen wall.

Mr Bateman looked up from his marking and smiled at Gethin; he smiled back and mouthed a silent greeting which Mr Bateman returned. Gethin put the dozen or so geography books back on their shelf and turned to talk to his teacher, but his head was already back in his books. With no reason to linger by the study area and insufficient courage to go up to Mr Bateman and ask if they could talk, he went to fetch the remaining pile of returns and went to the science section at the other end of the library.

For some weeks after his stay in Liverpool, Gethin had tried to prop up the screen which Jamie and Ste's story had so successfully toppled. The hikes and bike rides he and his friends had arranged made hiding from the dawning truths of his life easier, but he couldn't escape the knowledge that in all games of hide-and-seek, that which was hidden was always found. Then there had been the tense days leading up to the exam results, and those few exhilarating hours which high achievement and congratulation had brought. His course of A-level study was set, and before the trough of anti-climax swallowed him he got caught up in all the preparations for Enlli; ever since he could remember, the whole family had spent the week of August bank holiday on the remote island. Everyone had thought that this year would be different – that Seifion, Gethin's brother, wouldn't be able to come home from America; but then Seifion had phoned to say that his newspaper needed him back in London for the first week in September, so he'd be with them after all. For a whole week, Gethin packed all the provisions they'd need on the island into boxes which were then wrapped in black bin bags to keep everything dry during the trip in the open boat across the sound. At least this year they didn't have to take all their drinking water too!

Their week on Enlli was, for different reasons, special to each member of the family. His mother liked the peace and unhurried simplicity of life without electricity and phones, cars and supermarket queues – and patients! She'd sometimes come in from a walk and say things like *'Mae bywyd ar yr ynys 'ma yn gneud i rywun gwestiynnu daliadau'r oes gyfoes . . .* – Life here makes you question so much of what we think is important on the mainland . . . ', to anyone who happened to be in ear-shot, but such things were said in ways which beckoned only the responses of her own thoughts. Ann Jones would bake bread every day and gut the fish that Seifion caught in Bae'r Nant at the north end – things which Gethin never saw his mother do at home. His father spent hours alone reading and meditating; on his first visit to the island, more than thirty years ago, Llyr had found a sheltered cove near Pen Diben, at the south end beyond the lighthouse. It was to the cove that he retreated, drawn back by the whisperings of Beuno, Dyfrig, Padarn and other long-dead saints, to be with his thoughts and God. Seifion liked to fish for bass and pollack, and in the last years, since his work had taken him to places like Sarajevo and Grozny, he seemed to use his time on Enlli to find some peace inside himself; by the end of the week he'd be lamenting his choice of career in journalism and wishing he could stay. Eilir painted and enjoyed long talks with her mother; but mostly she painted. And for Gethin the island was where wonders unfolded. He watched grey seals and built dry stone walls; he looked, late into the night, for Manx Shearwaters in the beam of a torch and watched for the small flocks of Choughs. Over the years he'd talked with the marine biologists and the botanists, the geologists and the entomologists that stayed at the Bardsey Bird and Field Observatory and accompanied them on their field trips; for Gethin the island was a living encyclopaedia of the natural world.

On the evening before they crossed over to Enlli the whole family had lingered at the supper table. Eilir had unfolded the

saga of the last days of the fungus on the kitchen wall and
Seifion had told them stories about New York – the unbearable
August heat, the congestion and pollution caused by too many
cars, the crumbling health care system – about which he'd been
doing a piece for his newspaper . . . Then Eilir had talked about
her AIDS patient; Ann had wanted to know if they were using
the new combination therapy in Liverpool, the one she'd read
about in the *BMJ* . . . Seifion told the grim details of a visit to an
under-funded AIDS hospice, run by a group of nuns in Queens,
where people died in their own filth . . . Eilir couldn't speak
highly enough about the loyalty and care her AIDS patient's
partner had shown and how impressed she'd been with the
faithfulness of her patient's gay friends. 'Gwrywgydwyr ydy'r
grŵp sydd mewn perygl o hyd ta . . . – Homosexuals are still the
highest risk group then . . . ', Ann had said. Both Eilir and
Seifion tried to say something about how it was behaviours that
were risky, and that the notion of risk shouldn't be pinned onto
groups of people like a badge, but their words were lost as the
talk shifted from health care to homosexuality . . . Llyr didn't
believe that God was punishing homosexuals through this
disease, but that the disease was a consequence of their
sinfulness and the biggest lesson to humanity from the whole
AIDS crisis was that if we chose to flout God's law some pretty
catastrophic things would happen . . . Seifion talked about two
gay friends, one from university days and the other a journalist;
coming to know these two men had made Seifion re-think his
position – the position he'd grown up with – Llyr's position.
Seifion didn't think, any longer, that being gay was sinful . . .
And wasn't all the work with the human genome project going
to reveal that sexual orientation was genetically predisposed? If
that was true, then gay people were an intended part of God's
creation. Llyr had said that even if science did reveal the genetic
basis of sexual orientation, that didn't make homosexual acts
any less sinful; the Bible was clear that sexual intercourse
between a man and a woman in marriage was what had been

ordained; celibacy was the only acceptable lifestyle for homosexuals, as it was for all unmarried people.

Perhaps Gethin imagined that both his brother and sister had blushed on hearing this; he knew that he'd blushed as soon as they'd started talking about homosexuality. He'd thought that he might clear the table while they talked, to hide his anxiety and embarrassment, and yet, the things that Eilir and Seifion had said had been interesting and positive. Before falling asleep, he decided that he'd talk with Seifion in the morning when they drove together to Porth Meudwy at the tip of the Lleyn.

Waiting on the pebble beach for the two rowing boats to carry everyone and everything bound for the island across the bay to the larger boat in the anchorage, Gethin considered his disappointment. Who was he most disappointed in, himself or his brother? Seifion had said it was a phase that he'd pass through; he'd even shared with Gethin that he and two other boys, when they were about thirteen, had 'played' with themselves and had competitions to see who could do it quickest and shoot highest. When Gethin hadn't seemed convinced, Seifion talked about a sexual experience with a French boy during a language exchange when he was about Gethin's age; they'd shared the same room for the whole of Seifion's stay and done things in bed together; none of it had meant that he was gay. Gethin hadn't tried to explain what he knew to be true; but then – he didn't have the words to give it any shape, and alongside Seifion's experiences Gethin had nothing to share – just an intuitive knowing, without form or outline – without a voice.

Bugail Enlli rounded Pen Cristin and came into calmer water. The sound had been wilder than Gethin could remember and everyone was soaked. The two Germans left behind by the Observatory boat had sat next to him and in the first minutes of the crossing, in the relative calm of the Lleyn's lee, they'd introduced themselves. Gethin, filled with the confidence of his A*, had said 'Hallo! Mein Name ist Gethin Llyr'; he'd tried to explain that it would probably get rougher once they got into the channel and that it might be a good idea to wear the waterproofs that were tucked through the straps of their rucksacks. Bernd, the one Gethin supposed was about his own age, speaking in English that was better than Gethin's German, had said that it was his first time on such a small boat. When all the conversations had submitted to awe at the waves and silent prayers, Bernd wove his arm through Gethin's to stop himself being thrown around so much. Later, standing side by side on the uneven jetty in the Cafn, passing all the luggage from the boat along the line to the waiting tractor and trailer, Gethin and Bernd talked easily. The German boy was impressed that Gethin had been to the island every summer; he asked about its wonders. Did Gethin know about the Seal Cave . . . ? He'd read all about it; was it hard to find? Gethin said that it was, but that he'd take him there if he liked.

When Bernd came to Carreg Fawr later in the day to find Gethin, Ann Jones, who'd been kneading the first batch of dough, had tried to explain that she wasn't Mrs Llyr, but Mrs Jones – but that he could call her Ann anyway. Bernd, in his confusion, had said that in Germany it was impossible for children not to carry their parents' family name. Ann had done her best to explain that her three children were named according to an old Welsh tradition whereby sons were known as 'son of' and daughters as 'daughter of' – so Eilir was Eilir Ann and Gethin was Gethin Llyr. Though Gethin had gone fishing with Seifion and Ann didn't know for sure when they'd be back. Bernd stayed with her at Carreg Fawr and she told him stories about the island; he especially liked the idea that they might be stuck there for days if the weather turned bad. When Gethin and Seifion returned with three large pollack, more than enough for supper, Bernd and Gethin went to climb all 548 feet of Mynydd Enlli; from the 'mountain-top' Gethin could point out interesting places and give Bernd his bearings.

The hour after all the supper things had been cleared away

was quiet time. Gethin had never thought to question this, it was part of their life on Enlli; an hour in silence to listen for the wisdom of the twenty thousand saints and God. The last quarter of the quiet hour was evening prayer and they all came together in the small front room; sometimes this was silent too, and at other times someone would say whatever their day on the island moved them to say. Gethin thought about Bernd; when he'd put his arm through Gethin's, on the boat, he'd become aroused . . . He'd had an erection. The memory of it, now – before God, left him filled with shame. It would be hard to live as a homosexual in a world with God, Gethin thought, but how much harder might life be without God?

Eilir and Gethin were eating breakfast when Bernd turned up at Carreg Fawr. 'Today we explore the Seal's Cave, ja?' he'd asked. 'Wenn du willst,' Gethin had said . . . If you like! They put some bread and cheese in Bernd's ruck-sack and set off to explore the east side of the mountain. Ann shouted after them that they needed to be careful on the sheer slopes above the sound; the last thing she wanted was to scramble on the scree to tend broken legs!

From high up on the north side of the mountain Gethin spotted Seifion, fishing from a shoulder of rock in Bae'r Nant way off below them. As they came over to the east side they saw a man sunbathing; he mumbled something about being careful on the narrow paths. Across Cardigan Bay, Cader Idris proved a worthy throne for its mythical giant and the blue of the sea was spotted with bright sail-cloth. When the path dropped away steeply, Bernd betrayed the first clue that the expedition was more dangerous than he'd anticipated; 'You're sure this is the right way, Gethin? If we fall here then – das isses . . . !' Gethin reassured him and suggested that they ease themselves down the steep, scree path on their bottoms. After ten minutes they reached Seal Cave.

Bernd looked disbelievingly at Gethin . . . 'But this hole . . . It's too small . . . You're sure this is the place?' Gethin remembered that he had thought the same thing that first time with Seiifon. 'It's just the entrance that's small, then it opens out . . . ' And Gethin disappeared into the blackness with 'Come right behind me. You can hold on to my leg if you're frightened . . . 'And then he felt the German boy's hand around his ankle. Half way along the pitch black tunnel Gethin heard the wheezing and snorting of the seals echo from the underground chamber. He whispered into the darkness behind him that if they stayed as quiet as possible they wouldn't scare the seals. When they both finally pulled themselves from the tunnel onto the wide, flat rock and looked down into the cave, well-lit from a large jagged opening just below the water's surface, they saw two seals basking on the rocks just feet away and another deep in the water, an outline against the water-filtered light. They hardly dared to breathe and marvelled at the wonder of it all.

After ten, perhaps fifteen minutes, Bernd had asked, in a whisper, whether they could swim with the seals. Gethin remembered that he and Seifion had swum in the cave a few times, but that the seals were usually frightened off . . . 'We can try . . . ', Gethin whispered back. Bernd stood up and as he took off his clothes Gethin saw that his body was already that of a man. 'Come . . . Let's swim . . . ' he whispered, beckoning Gethin to undress. Gethin followed him into the water. The two basking seals snorted, wriggled from their rocks and dived deeply, circling them both before making for the under-water exit to the open sea. The boys were enthralled and hugged one another, each discovering the other's excitement. They swam together . . . Touching . . . Exploring one another's bodies . . . And they kissed . . . On the wide, flat rock above the water they lay in one another's arms for a long time, their bodies moving together. Bernd's sigh, when it finally erupted from somewhere deep inside him, echoed around the cave before dying away into Gethin's low moan.

During the quiet hour that evening Llyr told them the story of Saint Beuno and the curlew; he'd watched the birds for most of the afternoon, breaking off the legs of small crabs before swallowing them. According to the legend, Beuno, in the years before coming to Enlli to die, had lost his book of sermons overboard on a stormy sea crossing; in some despair, he arrived back at his cell in Clynnog Fawr to find his sermons, pulled from the sea and carried back to him by a curlew. It was a story Gethin had heard every summer on the island, but then, of Enlli's twenty thousand, Beuno was his father's favourite. Gethin's mind wandered to Bernd and to Seal Cave and now, before God, he wasn't so sure that it was the 'beautiful thing' it had been that afternoon.

Later, feeling heavy with a guilt that only Welsh Calvinism could bestow, Gethin left Carreg Fawr in search of some distraction. Near Ogof Hir he looked for Shearwaters. Beuno came to him . . . And then there were two others, perhaps Dyfrig and Padarn, but their faces were hidden under their hoods . . . And there were curlews; lots of curlews. Startled by the swiftness of their appearance, Gethin dropped his torch; the glass broke as it hit the rocks and the beam died. The blackness of the night wrapped itself around him and, through the curlew's melodic 'cur-lee', Beuno whispered his wisdom. Gethin didn't want to hear words of judgement and condemnation and he hit out at the three robed figures, shouting at them to leave him alone. Their robes and whisperings folded over and under him and, quiet in their embrace, he was carried back to Seal Cave. Beuno spoke through the whisperings of the other two in a babble of Latin and Welsh, Greek and Hebrew, and though it sounded odd, Gethin understood. Beuno wept for all the men down the centuries whose lives had been tortured by self-hatred because they had loved other men. 'The glory of God is the fully alive human being', he'd said, 'and as it is your providence to love men, love them well, in truth and faithfulness . . . Where love is true and faithful, God will dwell . . . *Ubi caritas et amor, Deus ibi est . . .* '

The bell rang and as Gethin watched Mr Bateman pack away his books he decided that his need to talk might keep until another day. They both reached the library door together and with a broad smile, Mr Bateman asked, 'Sut wythnos ges ti ar Enlli? – What sort of week did you have on Bardsey?' Gethin said he had a lot to tell and agreed to help set up some apparatus in the lab during the lunch break. And so Gethin got to talk.

Mr Bateman listened as Gethin explained that he now realised he was gay and understood that he needed some support, but he interrupted Gethin when he started to tell him about Bernd and the Seal Cave . . . 'I don't want to know if you've had sex with boys, Gethin; that would put me in a difficult position . . . ' And he explained about the school's policy on sex education and the laws which guided it; 'I'd be expected to inform the head if I knew that one of our pupils was having sex below the age of consent . . . And the school policy doesn't really give me much guidance on how to talk with you about gay issues . . . Can't you talk about this with someone else?' After a long silence Gethin said that he didn't think there was anyone else, but that he didn't want to put Mr Bateman in an awkward position either, and he left the lab feeling let down and lonely.

That evening, when the loneliness became too deep, Gethin told his parents he was gay. Ann said she'd ring one of the psychiatrists at the hospital. Llyr knew of a healing ministry on the Wirral that had some success in saving homosexuals. They both wanted the best for him. *Ubi caritas et amor, ubi caritas, Deus ibi est.*

Later that evening Kevin Bateman talked with his brother's lover, David, about what support he might offer Gethin; 'You could suggest that he phone the gay help-line in Bangor . . .' He then wrote Gethin a note to say that he was sorry for letting him down and he put the phone number David had given him clearly on the bottom . . . *Ubi caritas et amor, ubi caritas, Deus ibi est.*

The Woman Next Door

Angharad Price
Translated by Meic Stephens

The woman next door told me. She above all others persuaded me to renounce three things: my job in a large bank in London; my lover and colleague, George; and all other follies. I was summoned home by the death of my grandfather, and the need to put his things in order, and whether to keep or sell the house, Gorffwysfa. Ours was an ordinary and friendly village somewhere between Snowdonia and the sea. The people, in the main, were kind and considerate, and sometimes shy. There was a shop, two garages with petrol pumps – the village lay between two larger towns – three chapels and a primary school from the nineteenth century. Occasionally the chip-shop would re-open until we grew tired of potatoes and fat.

It had a Hebrew name: Bethlehem. I'd been brought up under the frown of Grandfather and neighbours on both sides. Bethlehem had been built by the quarry-owners in the heyday of the slate-industry. Few quarrymen were still alive; some had died of old age and the remainder of dust. Most of the children's fathers weren't quarrymen; nor was my grandfather. But, like Prince Charles himself, we'd observed in the museum the craft of extracting, splitting and loading slate. We walked along the track of the old quarry-line as far as the Menai Straits; we learned 'The Old Quarryman' by heart for the village eisteddfod; we went to Sunday School to give thanks and pray for those less fortunate, and on a trip to Rhyl in July.

The terrace was somewhat apologetic, puny – though not by choice – and aware of it. It snuggled back-to-back with a longer terrace. There was a Methodist chapel at the far end, also aware of its obscurity. We stooped on entering and squatted as we peered through the window in search of daylight.

The house on the corner was a shop. The owner – a stout, slow woman – kept a pigeon-loft opposite. She raced the birds on Saturday afternoons and their cooing was louder than hers. Sometimes children would pause on their way round the village and tease the birds – out of boredom. Another meeting place was the telephone box on the main road where we'd ring each other's houses without inserting coins. All this in a village which was otherwise quiet.

Gorffwysfa had two bedrooms – one for me, one for Grandfather. The beds in both were now empty, but in one bedroom lay Grandfather's coffin, waiting to be taken to Llanddeiniolen cemetery. Old Man's smells pervaded. I wouldn't be keeping Gorffwysfa. Strange to think: bricks and mortar were my only connection with home now. What were the people to me?

'Your grandfather left here in order to fill his soul with hope and despair.'

The woman next door rushed this sentence. She seemed disconcerted and was observing me. Gorffwysa was no longer the axis and she'd become a woman with no address. Having left next door, she'd become strange and real. Grey-eyed, her glance caressed all objects, and her skin was pale. There was a peace about her, not unlike the peace of the grave. She was a handsome woman but had never married, and now sought acknowledgement of those words.

'Grandfather was a hymn-writer,' I assured her.

'A hymn-writer and a psalmist, but with poetic aspirations.

As a youth he'd wandered the mountains of Snowdonia. Never really saw them, only heard rhymes in every echo.'

I nodded and confirmed: 'The Snowdon echo.'

'Yes. He left Snowdon's people to seek colours other than blue. It was a difficult thing to leave like that. People didn't in those days – they stayed put.'

'Just like today then.'

'No, it was different then!' the woman next door retorted, ceasing to look at me, bowing her head and seeming to stare at the sky beyond the quarry. 'You know nothing about the time before you're born.'

She'd always been quick-tempered and yet ready to forgive. Not surprising that many around here were jealous of her. I brought her back to her story by saying: 'Heaven is blue, isn't it? But living here between Snowdonia and the sea, Grandfather had nothing to compare it with. A spectrum of blue.'

'You're right, my girl.'

She caressed the space between us with a stroke of her hand, as if brandishing a paintbrush, dirtying an image in the air. Perhaps she did possess the artist's imprudent nature. Bold and splendid, she daubed truisms between the two of us, then used words to prevent the colours from fusing. 'Your grandfather possessed a triple conscience: that of the puritan, the poet and the Welshman. He left Bethlehem in order to lose himself, and took neither his religion nor his Welshness with him. No, he retained only one vocation, that of the poet, which bridged the gap between here and there.'

'Where did he go then?'

'He came to Tuscany . . . '

I'm sure the woman next door said 'came', but when she repeated herself, 'came' had changed to 'went'.

'Your grandfather went to Tuscany and discovered the lapis-lazuli ceilings of the cathedrals with their golden stars, calm and symmetrical. He fondled the breast of the Madonna, touching the body of her suckling child, felt the child's hand clutching his hand and heart. He discovered the black and white marble pillars in the churches of Siena and Lucca, marvelled at the colours of Giotto and Masaccio, sensed the pain and pleasure of going beyond, and desired it for himself. He delighted in Francis of Assisi's love of creatures. He cowered beneath Donatello's prophets as they challenged him to respond. He viewed Brunelleschi's red dome, felt the mystery of its brickwork and ribs. In the octagonal baptistry the devil was punishing sinners.

'Boys and girls in the street in sunglasses spoke in tongues. There was colour on their faces as they acted in the street's pageant.'

The woman next door paused. She removed the saliva from the corner of her mouth with finger and thumb, then swallowed.

'Your grandfather let go. He tasted of the plums and olive-trees in the orchards, and of the juices in the fields. It left a sweet green taste in his mouth, familiar to Tuscans. He drank deep of the red wine of Montalcino.'

But Grandfather had never been a drinker. He'd frowned on the villages. On hearing them singing hymns past our house on Saturday nights and early on Sunday morning he would gulp down his tea, clenching the cup in his fist.

'I'm sorry, but I'll have to interrupt. Grandfather didn't drink. Stop lying at once, before I lose my temper.'

She'd made me very angry with her gossip. But to avoid a quarrel with the woman next door, who was strangely calm, I added:

'What I mean is that I can't recall Grandfather taking strong drink. Can you blame me for defending him in his absence?'

'May I proceed?'

'By all means.'

And the woman next door proceeded. I relaxed and leant back against the chair, listening for any sound from the bedroom where the coffin lay.

160

'Drinking deep of Montalcino's finest wines, his thirst was such that no one could quench it. Your grandfather's lips were stained with Brunello wine, his teeth and tongue the colour of blue slate, redness mixed with the sun's freckles on his nose. It was the redness of flowing blood; he never touched the colourless Grappa.

'Your grandfather was a handsome man, as I said, intent on becoming a poet and experimenting with colour and sound. Helpless and charming, he knew when to laugh and when to sulk, and when subtly to mention his own innocence. He handled the women well, yes, he learned how to love when he left here for Italy.'

When the woman next door finally paused her colours still hung in the air, filling our house, Gorffwysfa, spreading over the plain walls, dripping onto Grandfather's bookcase, over the books, forming puddles on the carpet which finally absorbed them.

I was angry with her again on account of the mess she'd made. In truth, her story was familiar. It was my story.

'Shame on you, ridiculing Grandfather like that! What do you know about him that I don't?'

'What does anyone know about anyone?' she muttered.

'Everyone knows everything about everyone around here.'

'So they say.'

'And knows nothing at the same time,' I concurred despite myself, for the woman next door and I were, in the end, rather similar. 'If Grandfather was far away, the Snowdon echo couldn't have known anything, let alone report it. And he never told me about any of that, which is strange as we were so close.'

This was a jibe.

'It was a hot day,' she interrupted. It was difficult not to admire her for her perseverance.

There she was again with her coarse paintbrush, showing up the space between us by filling it with colour: a thick pink stripe here under the lamp; a yellowish-red circle like the yolk of an egg, like the setting sun; a dab of black hovering over Grandfather's clock; a square ruby hanging under her right ear like an earring. She drew an egg shape in gold, pushing it away with the handle of the brush until it came to stand in front of Grandfather's favourite painting – that of the old woman of Salem with the devil in her shawl. The woman next door was having fun painting and laughing at the same time. Her face creased as she enjoyed herself.

The colours were familiar. Nicer to have them in Gorffwysfa than not to have them at all. They were alive, and made a mess of the house and furniture. They filled everywhere. She was welcome to her fun. I refrained from getting upset.

'Is this a new story?'

'A new slant on the old. Hold your tongue and listen, young lady,' she scolded. 'It was a hot day at the convent of San Antimo near Montalcino. Your grandfather was dying of hunger and thirst. Food and drink were provided by the convent for anybody in need. He was unwilling and proud, but faint when he reached the door, suffering from too much wine; his lips were dry and cracked. He was put to bed and looked after for two or three days, I can't be sure. The white nuns of San Antimo all loved him secretly. Who could blame them? And he too loved being there.

'He claimed that he would immortalize them in his poetry. Of course, only God can bestow immortality, but there were those on earth who worked on God's behalf: poets and other artists, for instance. This too pleased your grandfather. He recovered unwillingly.

'He ate in a cool room beneath the refectory. Through the window was the yellow and dark-green Tuscan landscape. He'd been set aside on account of his sex, that's to say, because he was a man. He felt a bit sorry for himself, no doubt.

'A girl from the village, not the nuns, served his food. She was pretty and very young. They knew almost at once that they were aiming for the same place.

'Only gradually did they draw closer. She was wary of the foreigner with his strange lilt – it was said that he wasn't an Englishman – he was altogether more impetuous. But he held back, anxious not to rush things, and feared the gloom after she'd left when he tried to sleep and recover. Slowly, in that cool room, they became acquainted. They would have twenty minutes at a time and weren't supposed to speak. Nor did they, at first.

'For him she was a saint, an angel at least. She shone in the darkness of the room, especially at evening, as if illuminated by the setting sun. He saw in her face the features of Mary. After she'd gone he remembered the curve of her thigh. The stranger's skin was pale, his shoulders broad, and he had long sturdy legs; he was more like a statue than the local boys.

'They smiled and then spoke, holding each other's gaze and blushing a bit. Talking was a relief, the words conducting the heat from their bodies and into the landscape. They would talk about everyday things. Fearing she would ask about here, he did most of the talking. She gleaned things from the silences without his knowing, and from the movements of his body as he ate. She came closer, sometimes accepting some food. Leftovers were sent back to the kitchen and this caused raised eyebrows. Anna had black eyebrows and black hair, tied back.

'There was no going back. Still cautious, they hadn't touched each other. He was oddly reserved. She was too beautiful. Your grandfather feared losing control. Wasn't poetry his first love? But one day Anna bent over him and her body was smooth as a sickle. Touching was a shock. Her breast was softer than the marble breasts of the effigies. As they kissed the world turned around . . .'

The woman next door suddenly fell silent. I looked up and froze as she groaned loudly. And then I saw myself in her.

It was a long time before she went on with her story. I wasn't listening any more.

'Your father finally came back and you with him . . . '

'What did you say?'

'Your grandfather came back and you with him as a baby. Soon afterwards I moved in next door. He brought you up here. It was in Gorffwysfa and in Bethlehem that his soul was filled with hope and despair, with you. The words never came again to conduct the heat from his body, nor did they bring it in. What did this blue landscape have to offer except something hard and cold? He forgot everything as he brought you up, attempting to salve two-thirds of his triple conscience. Such poetry as he wrote was lullabies for you. The story was known to all, except you.'

'Stop it!'

And the woman next door stopped. Her voice was hoarse anyway, and the words had failed to prevent the colours from congealing into one another, forming a rust-red smudge. But before she withdrew again to next door, I had one more question. It didn't embarrass her: 'Why did you never marry?'

'I've been through love and come out the other side. Why marry, except . . . ?'

'Except what?'

'Except to have children.'

She threw back her head, looked at me and parted the colours which were a mess between us.

'I'll see you tomorrow at Grandfather's funeral.'

'We'll stand closest to him, as it was when he was alive. You in London and me next door.'

I could have run after the woman next door and stabbed her with the handle of the paintbrush, but decided not to. Strange that nobody had said anything. Perhaps the pigeons had cooed loud enough. And as if she were reading my mind, the woman next door turned and called: 'I was closest to him, not you!'

Our house was not sold after all. I came back to Bethlehem to correct my memories. Gorffwysfa was still apologetic. Sometimes I have chips. Occasionally I send letters to my friends from the post-box near the shop on the corner, mostly to

164

George in London. It gives me something to do.

I live by painting pictures on pieces of old slate. Quotations from psalms or verse by local poets, with coloured patterns. They're sold as souvenirs in the museum at Llanberis. Sometimes I daub paint all over the house.

I shan't move away until the woman next door dies. Haven't I some responsibility towards her? Even then, I might not leave. Because then I'll be the woman next door for others. But it was she who showed me how easy it is to lose yourself here. The woman next door taught me to paint camouflage over the house and over myself. It was here, in fact, that I turned blue. Inside me flows the red of Montalcino wine.

Of Rocks and Stones

Tristan Hughes

It was late in January and the Reverend Edward Morris was sitting at the desk in his study, watching through his window as successive banks of cloud swooped in from the sea, slowing to crawl over the Orme and Ynys Seiriol, before stopping momentarily to lower over his roof and deposit their seemingly bottomless supply of rain upon it. The wind that drove them was veering uncertainly, sending the waves below first this way and then that, churning the surface of the water into a blizzard of baffled white crests. This time of year he tended to take the weather personally – everyone did. There was always an edge in January to what might otherwise seem merely perfunctory observations about climatic conditions – a feeling that their malignity was aimed directly at you, was summoned for the specific purpose of wearing down your already frayed spirit, to make sure that before spring came you would be well and truly beaten. Conversations about the weather in January were a perilous business, Morris had realised, because there was always a hint of blame directed against him, as though somehow he were complicit in it, had worked it all out with the creator he was supposed to represent as a cruel test of faith. He could see it in their eyes, the suspicion. And there was nothing he could do to dispel it, because whatever mysterious ways impelled these clouds to descend like the lid of a cauldron in November and remain until May, he was not able to explain, or indeed justify them, to men. Besides, he was a victim of it as much as they were, and took his place each season in the assembled ranks of island Jobs.

He'd spent the morning trying to write a letter to his brother in America. He attempted this at least once a year, invariably at some point in mid-winter. So far he'd completed two in ten years, but had never sent any. What actually compelled him to begin them in the first place remained something of an enigma to him. He had not seen or spoken to his brother, who taught geography in a college somewhere in Florida (he had not quite reached the point of memorising an address), for ten years or more, which was an awfully long time – long enough, certainly, to explain his compulsion as guilt. But it didn't feel like guilt. There were just days when the ring of mountains and sea outside his window began to tighten slightly, an infinitesimal contraction, but one that made him restless and fidgety as though he were chafing against some invisible constraint. And then, almost without willing it, he would find himself here at his desk, pen in hand, scribbling to a brother he had nigh on forgotten, not really knowing what he was saying or why he was saying it. In return for his unfinished letters he received, at Christmas, a page written by his brother's American wife, describing what 'we' had done this year, a collective pronoun that included their two sons, a Labrador and two cats; sometimes he was interested in what the cats had done, but only sometimes.

Today's letter had begun quite gloomily – how could he help it with half the Irish Sea cascading down his drain pipes and the rest, apparently, sweeping in from the grey horizon – in a style he feared was a bit stilted and self-indulgent (his brother had little time for flowery prose, he had always preferred bold, uncluttered lines that did not deviate as they passed over the terrain beneath: longitudes, latitudes). Dear William, it began:

Another long winter to suffer through. The rectory has decided to let in more of God's breath this year, which sweeps through the rooms with all the desolate aplomb of an old testament lament. Or perhaps these drafts are just the ghosts of chilly sermons past, come back from the deceased mouths of my predecessors to haunt me. All this must seem very remote to you these days, ensconced, as I imagine you to be, on a pleasant porch, swathed in tropical sunshine and drinking mint juleps. I doubt you can have too many regrets about leaving – there was so little for you here. I think about you often (sometimes) though. Yesterday I walked to the beach down past Cucu's place, the one with the white stones (I suppose it's all white sand over there), to look at the rock pools we used to catch shrimps in when we were boys. They have hardly changed at all, although the beach itself is a bit different. The council, or the National Trust, I can't be sure which, has built a parking lot at the top of the cliff and the old path that went down through the ferns has been replaced by a fancy new track made of wood and gravel. There are more people too, mainly fishermen from Liverpool, and more rubbish; mostly plastic bags, that hang like a foul drapery off the orange bracken. I actually tried to catch a few shrimps but they easily eluded me (I'm not quite so sprightly as I was back then), and instead grazed my hand on a very ancient looking limpet, which was itself encrusted with barnacles, as though it had been there for so long that it had become mistaken for the rock it clung to. I wondered if it had been there since we were children, if maybe it had grazed me before. I know it might sound odd, but afterwards I felt a certain affinity with this old limpet, clinging for a whole lifetime to one small piece of rock, in one small pool, on one small beach. Because haven't I, in a way, been doing exactly the same thing. Yes, of course, my Rock may well be larger – in both a spiritual and geographical sense – but isn't it possible that my horizons have perhaps been correspondingly bounded, that I have looked up at the surface of my pool, through the water darkly, and imagined I looked on the whole world, when all the time I was straining my eyes to glimpse only the merest fragment of it. I have never been married, I have never had children. I have never lived anywhere but here on this small island that

And yet what, he thought, pausing with his pen and looking down over the broad expanse of white that remained below the ink. Outside the window a cloud had stopped on the opposite shore of the straits and lay, exhausted, beneath the round summit of Carnedd Dafydd. He put his pen down on the desk, picked up the piece of paper, and was just on the point of depositing it in the bin when a knock on the door diverted him. It was Gwynfor Owen, who owned the garage in the village. He had obviously come straight from work and there were smears of black oil on his forehead and cheeks; droplets of rain clung to his silver hair and occasionally fell down onto his face, slithering off the oil and sliding down his neck. He looked as though coming to the Reverend Morris's house was the last thing he would have chosen to do and that this visit had weighed heavily upon him for the whole morning. There were pinched, determined creases at the corners of his eyes. It took a while for him to speak, which was not unusual because Gwynfor didn't like to speak much, and when he did, each utterance was short and blurted, spluttering rapidly into silence like a faulty car ignition.

'Sorry to bother you Mr Morris.'

'Not at all Gwynfor. What can I do for you?'

'It's Catrin. I wondered if you'd come by and see her.'

'That's no problem, Gwynfor, but why does she want to see me?'

'She's not herself.'

'What, you mean she's sick? Have you got the doctor around yet?'

'It's not like that Mr Morris.' Morris was about to ask how it was then exactly, or what it was at least, but Gwynfor was quite evidently at the very limit of his conversational reserves – the strained creases besides his eyes were deepening into rifts and canyons – and so he just said fine, he'd come around first thing in the evening.

As he watched Gwynfor walk back towards his car a gust of wind rippled over the confused waters of the straits, lifting up the resting cloud and driving it onwards, where it shattered on the peaks of Foel Goch and Mynydd Perfedd.

* * *

As the darkness began to fall the sky became clearer and the wind became colder. He walked along the road that led from the old priory and Seiriol's well into the village. The waves, which by now had steadied themselves and found their true direction, lashed the sea wall to his left, sending clumps of chilly foam rolling across the tarmac. He made his way around to where the road touched the edge of Traeth Lleiniog, where spectral cliffs of sandstone crumbled into the sea, leaving strange shaped remnants beached on the shore. A pale and sodden moon heaved itself above the adjacent mountains and then vanished as he moved beneath the branches of the glen. Here a path opened up through the trees and he took it, lifting his feet carefully over the knotted, Gordian roots that sprawled across the ground in the shadows. To his surprise he found himself still speaking to his brother:

And yet isn't it also true that sometimes the most limited vantage point offers the widest view. You do not need to stand on the summit of Pisgah to see the world. A hard point to make nowadays, I know, when everyone, or so it seems, has travelled to the four corners of it. Whenever I talk to my parishioners they are always recounting the peripatetic exploits of restless sons, daughters and grandchildren, toing and froing from places I have only ever seen in photographs in that heap of National Geographics in the dentist's waiting room. But when they come back are they not still as young as I was at their age? You can have memories of the entire globe and very little understanding of any of it. The limpet never moves an inch but, over time, whole oceans will wash over it. Do you remember . . .

His foot stopped suddenly, though he did not remember willing it to stop, and the rest of his body had not seemed to make the necessary adjustment, its momentum pushing over it and heaving itself onto the muddy ground. One of the roots had downed him. He lay there for a second, looking up at the branches above him and the sky beyond them, seeing blackness etched across darkness.

His ankle was hurt, there was no doubt about it, but how badly hurt he wasn't sure. It still moved, a good sign. He was amazed that he'd fallen. How many times had he walked this way, during the day and the night. He'd thought he knew each obstacle, or at least that his feet did. It should have been instinct by now. He felt somehow betrayed – by his feet, by the track. But there was nothing else to do but hobble on, and so he did, until finally two orange lights appeared in front of him. As he approached them the track merged once more into tarmac and the branches receded into thin, umbrageous wisps. Houses began to take shape alongside of him and he could make out the weak lights that spread through forlorn, January kitchens, which everyone had vacated to hide around living room fires and the comforting glow of televisions, where palm trees swayed and people had skin as soft and clear as peaches. Soon he'd arrived beneath the streetlamps, that stood like sentinels at the bottom of the road that led up the hill through the village. Just beyond the pools of sad orange that oozed onto the ground around them, he could make out a small group of children huddled around the bus shelter, hiding precious cans of lager and stolen cigarettes. As he walked past they crowded furtively into the shelter, seeking out the deeper shadows, careful not to look up at him as they moved. In the daytime he'd probably have recognised them all, but now, in the night, the only one he could be sure of was Jack Tatws, whose father owned a field of potatoes behind his house. Jack, he remembered, had once

171

played the big xylophone in a harvest festival concert in the church, put on by the village primary school. They were the ones he always noticed, those ones whose fingers were not subtle enough for recorders or guitars, whose ears could not pick up a tune, and so instead were handed big sticks with felt heads and left to go about their asynchronous thumping like monkeys in a circus beating toy drums. He liked their solitary persistence, their frantic and smiling oblivion amongst rhythms and melodies that must have sounded to them as distant and unattainable as the planetary symphony conducted in the spheres.

He carried on up the hill, flanked by terraces, until he reached the brow, where he stopped to sit on a wall and rest his ankle. It was hurting quite badly now. Beside him was the local Spar shop and opposite it a large square building with a sharp triangular roof. It was called Bethania and had been a chapel until just after the war – when maybe the local people had begun to realise that they'd built a chapel or two too many, that they didn't have quite as many souls now to fill them, that their presence hadn't done too much to stop what had happened – but had now, after years of dereliction, been converted, optimistically, into holiday flats. Looking at it he wasn't sure whether he shouldn't feel a certain glimmer of satisfaction to see this evidence of the decline in nonconformist fortunes; but, considering the paltry level of attendance in his church, he thought it best not to. Besides, he liked this building, whose bold grey stones had somehow managed to avoid the rash of pebble-dash that seemed to afflict every other house in the village; it made them appear older, more enduring, and in the daylight, if you looked closely, you could see the unmistakable swirl of fossils embedded in them. They made him wonder how ancient they actually were – pre-Cambrian, Ordovician, antediluvian (which put him on safer ground, theologically speaking) – and how the great rifts and schisms they had witnessed, tectonic, geological, must have made those religious

172

ones that had necessitated them being dynamited and broken up and carted here, seem the merest trifles – ripples and tremors all.

A semi-circle of light appeared suddenly in front of Spar's doorway, and into it stepped Mrs Evans, carrying a red cotton bag (she didn't use the plastic shop ones) out of which poked a magazine and a newspaper. The Reverend Morris leapt instantly to his feet, thinking there was still time to slip behind the shop and avoid the conversation that he knew was coming; but, though he had been contemplating the drift of continents, he realised that shifting himself had become quite difficult. Dragging his ankle behind him, he'd got no further than the edge of the wall before he heard her voice: 'Well hello Mr Morris, and what brings you out this evening?' There was no escaping now.

Mrs Evans was one of his many slightly elderly female parishioners, of whom there were so many that he sometimes wondered if Welsh women actually died at all, if instead they were granted some kind of afterlife in this world, where they could harass their vicars as far down the corridors of eternity as it was humanly possible to go. None of them, however, was quite so pertinacious and voluble as Mrs Evans. Through the cold wind that spun in circles around the street, lifting up sweet wrappers and swirling them up into the night past the flapping wires of the electricity poles, she began to deliver a long and wearying jeremiad. Its subject was the degenerate elements who were swamping the locality, and its single example seemed to be the presence, in one of Cucu's fields, of two new age types who lived in a caravan. Morris, nodding assent at what he took to be the correct intervals, looked down and watched as his hands began to turn red and then purple. He was used to this, although he still wondered sometimes what exactly the likes of Mrs Evans wanted from him. Was it just a captive (and by now frozen) ear? No, he knew it was more – there was always Mike Spar and Dylan Post just for that – knew how on one level what they wanted was for him to lock their insights into a Christian embrace, to rubber stamp their prejudices and grievances and fears with the imprimatur of holy authority, to assure them that the errant BT repairman would face the very highest justice, to make it plain that God himself looked extremely poorly upon the recent defacement of the bus shelter. And, in a better temper and on warmer days, he could understand this need. Judgements and apprehensions and frustrations were a lonely business, why shouldn't they seek out companionship, and His companionship at that? And he could understand as well the downward slant of much of these laments. He was old himself. What could be more natural than to see reflected in the world around you the evidence of that decay to which you yourself were subject, to view alteration through the lens of disintegration; why shouldn't eyes that were failing see failure? It was an anthropomorphic folly, of course, an almost profane equation, but it was instinct too, the same as any other animals need to build a shelter around itself, where it could live, or die. What he couldn't understand, in Mrs Evans' case at least, were the particular snobberies that muddied these waters. Why should she single out two hippies who'd dragged a caravan into a field for her opprobrium and, at the same time, praise what that man Giles had done just above them, vandalising the old windmill – would no one allow these poor rocks to rest – turning it into some Disney-gothic monstrosity? What made the one seem like the wrinkles on her skin and the other like plastic surgery? By the time she'd finished he was despondent.

. . . the times we used to walk along the cliff tops, all the way from Penmon to Traeth Coch, past the old quarries at Caim and Dock, over Y Fedw and under Bwrdd Arthur, and down onto those wide sands that never were red. It used to seem like the longest journey ever made. And nain would make sandwiches and barley water to provision us, enough to last us to the ends of the earth, and we'd carve boughs of hazel as swords and walking sticks, hacking our way through armies *of nettles, bramble battalions. Do you remember passing the mad old man who lived in Maes y Mor, Glyn-Ding-a-Ling, who skulked in his garden, waiting for us to steal his apples, and then rushed after us, as big as a Cyclops, waving his knotted cane above his head like a war club. Do you remember sitting on the rocks of Chwalar Wen, looking hard at the skyline, seeing if we could see the outline of the Isle of Man and pretending we could see Ireland and you said it was America and I said nobody could see that far. I still wonder when all of this began to shrink for you, when the flurry of childish steps became the merest Brobdingnagian stride, when all those horizons we couldn't see became no more than the name on a one-way ticket, when this bounded circle of shore became the constraining hoop that you had to jump through, and then beyond. When did it all come to seem too little, and then not enough. Sometimes I think . . .*

As she moved off down the pavement he watched as the wind pulled strands of greying hair out from under the edges of a wooden scarf that she had tied ever so carefully about her head.

* * *

Gwynfor Garage's garage was at the top of the village, just beyond a football pitch where several sheep were huddled beneath a rusty pair of goalposts. It looked like a house, like any other of the houses that stood beside it, with their flecks of gravel – a mixture of myriad shades of grey – clinging to their walls, only its bottom floor had been turned into a wide door of corrugated metal, that each morning slid open to reveal a bewildering array of twisted steel carcasses that seemed to have been there for so long that it was easy to imagine that Gwynfor's had become some kind of automobile's graveyard, a place where moribund motors, hearing their death rattles, crawled into so they might join the corroded bones of their forbears. Outside, on the forecourt, there were two petrol pumps, although these had been out of use for such an age that even amongst the whitest beards in the village there was still some debate as to whether there had ever been a time when they actually dispensed anything. Occasionally, particularly in the spring, visitors to the island, passing through the village, would stop their cars beside these pumps and wait for a small eternity until finally Gwynfor himself would shuffle out, responding to their requests for fuel with a baffled taciturnity, like a farmer who'd been asked the origin and purpose of the mouldering cromlechs in his field. He leaned for a moment on one of these, gathering thoughts which the wind had begun to scatter, smelling the coal smoke that careered down the roof slates towards him and then shuttled off along the street towards the dark fields beyond. He wondered why Gwynfor had called for him, what could be wrong with his wife? Over the years he had become used to making unusual house calls, whose purposes were as often as not only loosely contained within the purview of matters spiritual. In the past he had been the adjudicator in family conflicts, the comforter and advisor of pregnant, husbandless girls, the assuager of angry fathers, the rebuker of godless sons. Most often, in the days before GP's prescribed things for sadness, he had acted as a kind of doctor for the melancholy (the indigenous affliction, that seeped through the streams here, that saturated the very air), an unofficial post requiring of him long hours in silent, stricken kitchens, where he tried his best to smooth over the inexplicability, the awkwardness, the sheer embarrassment, of despair. Because so often there was no cause – no skeleton falling out of the closet, no lowering of coffins, no note on the table and bloody mess in the bathroom – only a waking up to find that same square of garden and bundle of bushes and rickety wooden fence that had sat outside your window all your life had suddenly become the most hopeless prospect in the entire world, a landscape sedimented with layer upon layer of futility and sorrow, as if everything you had ever lost, or never had, was fossilised in it. And afterwards the befuddled, stuporous immobility, as though you had sunk beneath thick, clammy oceans, with people's voices sounding weakly from a thousand fathoms above and you down here where the sunlight would never reach and the water clogged your lungs and the grey weeds wrapped themselves around your useless limbs. No cause, and when it happened how could you explain, and how could the rest of them understand. So they would call the Reverend Edward Morris, who would troop off through the rain on nights such as this, and try to make things a bit easier, a bit less strange, less extraordinary, as though only an exegete of miracles could drag it, gasping, into the cold light of day.

Looking up at the floral curtains on the second floor, lit up faintly from within, he hoped it would not be anything like this. In his memory there were rooms that felt infectious; places where the air made his skin prickle and whispered voices felt hot and humid like malarial breezes, wan figures crouched leper-like in corners. He felt too old now to be immune from it, as though all the antibodies of hope and belief and persistence that had shielded him once were drying up – thin, friable strands floating abandoned in his blood. He hoped it would not be this.

* * *

Three knocks and the door was open. Gwynfor produced a grunt that passed for a greeting and led him through into the kitchen, where the two of them stood in a windless silence, Gwynfor looking down at the gleaming linoleum floor while Morris surveyed the walls. There was a picture of their son, Will, a giant of a boy, trapped uncomfortably in a school uniform that clung precariously to his precociously bulging body, and beside it a tea cloth decorated with green hills and an Irish flag, inscribed with a proverb that ended with the line 'May the wind always be at your back', which right now Morris very much wished to be the case. On the opposite wall there was a painting, although painting did not really describe it, it was more a tableau vivant, in which a huge waterfall – he couldn't tell

177

which one – cascaded from the edge of a forested plateau. The water itself seemed to be made out of ridged and striated white plastic, through which a sequence of lights glowed, ebbing downwards and crashing onto the rocks beneath. Morris watched it for some time, struck by how easily transfixed he was by this cheap and gaudy illusion of movement. It was a good few minutes before he looked down and realised that his clothes were covered in mud. Feeling embarrassed suddenly he tried making conversation with Gwynfor.

'Terrible weather we're having,' he said.

'Yes,' Gwynfor replied, darting out a faintly accusing look. Meanwhile, the mud was becoming an ever more insistent question and Morris was greatly relieved when Gwynfor finally asked it.

'You have a fall?'

'No, not really. Just a tumble.' Gwynfor nodded his head. And just at that moment, which was an even greater relief, Catrin walked into the room.

She arrived speaking, as though she had already begun warming up in the corridor outside. Small and squat, with an air of perpetual motion about her, she always gave the impression that she was half way through at least five or six separate conversations, which she was obliged to shift her attention quickly between, balancing them like a juggler.

'Well, Mr Morris, isn't it lovely to see you. Hasn't Gwynfor got you some tea yet, Duw, I'll get it myself then. What he does all day down in that garage I don't know. I was telling Mair today, I see these cars go in there but I never see them coming out. And she says it's the same with her Idris, going out on his tractor all day and her not seeing any difference in the fields afterwards, and I said no it's hard to tell what they're doing, and she says well it's probably better not to know, only they come back in the evening moaning like nobody's business. So how are you? What Gwynfor's up to dragging you out on a night like this is beyond me, really it is, and I told him not to, told him it wouldn't make a blind bit of difference, only be a trouble for you and everything, and there he goes and does it, doesn't he. And look at you, covered in mud poor thing.'

At which point she whisked his coat out of his hand and probably would have started washing it there and then if the kettle hadn't begun to boil. Morris always thought how apt it was that these two had married each other, how otherwise there would simply have not been enough room in the house for all their words. Having expected the worst, Catrin's cheery volubility began to reassure him. Maybe they just wanted to donate something for the spring raffle? Whatever the case, he knew he wouldn't have to wait long to find out: Catrin would get to it soon enough. He was surprised how soon. As the table in front of him filled with cups and saucers, plates heaped with shortbread and biscuits, he listened to what he would never have expected: 'And I said to him, there's no use in trying to stop me, I've made up my mind and that's that. I've made the arrangements: Angharad and her husband are expecting me and they've said I can live with them as long as I want because the house is too big for just the two of them anyway, although why they'd want a house that big in the first place I don't know, but they're cheaper in Spain I suppose so why not have one with four bedrooms instead of just the two. But no, he won't get it into his thick head that I'm leaving, and Esgob Mawr I've told him enough times that I am. So what does he do but go about trying to get everyone in the village to have a talk with me, like that was going to change anything. I've made up my mind and that's that and God almighty isn't going to persuade me otherwise.' The Reverend Morris didn't know what to say.

But he had to say something. Gwynfor was looking utterly helpless, his shoulders slumping almost to the edge of the table, his face contorted with the effort to get out the words that wouldn't come – it was the one time in all his sixty years that he had something he really wanted to say, and he couldn't. So Morris said them: 'But Catrin, this has been your home for forty years, and you've always lived in the village.'

'That's what I've bloody well been trying to tell her!' Gwynfor gasped, the effort of it throwing him back into his chair. Catrin hardly blinked an eye.

'Well that's my point exactly Mr Morris, though you'd think it was rocket science the way it bounces off his bloody skull. I've been here for as long as I remember and one morning I just wake up and I'm thinking I'm not staying any more, I'm not going to sit around like one of those old buckets of rust downstairs, waiting till I'm nothing but dirt and dust. I don't have to. I'm thinking it's not like I'm some heap of stones stuck forever on the ground – I can get on a plane and go. I've life enough in me yet you know.'

* * *

. . . that at a certain point our vision somehow forked, like two roads splitting apart, and that you started wanting views that were horizontal, that unfolded sideways into space, when the only vistas here were vertical, slanting down into time, and those were mine. But what if I was wrong. What if all along it was me who wanted the wide horizon, to have prairies beneath my feet instead of graveyards, fields without walls, to walk as far as I wanted, without turning or veering, and not fall into the ocean. Because there are times now when the smallest crack in the clouds is enough to set my heart racing, when the feel of the wind on my back conjures continents, when the smallest raindrop on my window expanse is like the Pacific. And have you ever noticed how rock pools, when the tide is down, and the sea seems far away, look like the loneliest places in the world . . .

The night was dark and he was tired and his foot was hurting. Sitting down on a stone beside the road he looked into the blackness, unable to see anything, unable to move anywhere, not knowing how far away his home was.

Notes on Contributors

Kate Roberts (1891-1985) is acknowledged as the greatest Welsh language fiction writer of the twentieth century. She was born in Rhosgadfan and educated at the University College of North Wales Bangor. Following a period as a teacher in South Wales she married Morris Williams and together they became active in the field of publishing when they took over Gwasg Gee at Denbigh. An author of both novels and short stories; some of her work is now available in translation.

W.J. Gruffydd (1881-1954) was born at Bethel in Caernarfonshire, the son of a quarryman. He was educated at Caernarfon County School and Jesus College, Oxford and became a distinguished and much respected figure in the literary and political life of Wales. His work embraced poetry, drama, the essay, translation work and the editorship of *Y Llenor*, in which 'Distyll y Dail' *(Dripping Leaves)* first appeared.

Brenda Chamberlain (1912-1971) was born in Bangor and in 1931 commenced her training at the Royal Academy Schools. Following her marriage to fellow artist John Petts they lived at Llanllechid, near Bethesda. Later she abandoned painting in favour of poetry. The marriage ended in 1946 and not very long afterwards she moved to live on Bardsey *(Ynys Enlli)* but later moved to the Greek island of Ydra.

Her account of the rigours and excitement of life on Bardsey is the subject of 'Tide Race', which has now assumed the status of a Welsh classic.

John Gwilym Jones (1904-1988) was born at Groeslan in Gwynedd and studied at the University of North Wales before becoming a teacher. He was a producer with the BBC in Bangor for a time and was later offered a post as lecturer in Welsh at the University.

Although he wrote short stories, two novels and literary criticism he will probably be best remembered as a dramatist. Indeed he has been described as one of the two major Welsh language dramatists of the twentieth century, the other being Saunders Lewis.

Emyr Humphreys (1919-) was born in Prestatyn but moved to the nearby village of Trelawnyd at an early age. He was educated at Rhyl Grammar School and the University of Wales, Aberystwyth. In 1965 he took up a post as a lecturer in the drama department at the University of North Wales. Later he decided to become a full time writer and his resulting fictional output made his name in and outside Wales. Many of his novels are set in his native north-east Wales while others are set elsewhere, Italy for example. *Outside the House of Baal* is frequently referred to as possibly his finest achievement. He has also written poetry and drama and his book *The Taliesin Tradition* blends history and literature. He now lives in Llanfairpwll.

Alun T. Lewis (1905-1989) was born in Llandudno and became a teacher in Llanrwst for many years. His literary reputation rests entirely in the short story genre and he published three collections.

Eigra Lewis Roberts (1939-) was born in Blaenau Ffestiniog and educated at the University of North Wales. Her literary output has encompassed the novel, short fiction and drama. She is the author of a play in which the hymn writer Ann Griffiths is the central character. She lives in Dolwyddelan.

Jane Edwards (1939-) grew up in Newborough and was educated partly at the Normal College at Bangor. She is the author of a number of works of fiction and these are largely concerned with the complexities of adult relationships.

She is married to Derec Llwyd Morgan and lives at Aberystwyth.

Siân James (1932-) was born at Llandysul and educated at the University of Wales at Aberystwyth, and was granted an honorary doctorate by them two years ago. Following a period as a teacher in London she made her home in the Cotswolds having married the Shakespearean actor Emrys James.

She has been in the forefront of Welsh fiction writing in English for a number of years. Her novel *A Small Country* is now regarded as a twentieth century classic. She is also the author of a charming childhood memoir *The Sky Over Wales*.

Glenda Beagan (1948-) was born in Rhuddlan and studied at the University of Wales, Aberystwyth later obtaining an MA in Creative Writing at Lancaster. Her work has been widely anthologised and she has published two short story collections *The Medlar Tree and Changes and Dreams* and a volume of poems *Vixen*.

Robin Llywelyn (1958-) was born in Bangor and educated at the University of Wales, Aberystwyth. He writes both novels and short stories. His first novel *Seren Wen ar Gefndir Gwyn* appeared in 1992 and baffled certain reviewers because of its surreal nature.

He is a grandson of Sir Clough Williams-Ellis and is Managing Director of Portmeirion, the Italianate village near Penrhyndeudraeth.

Peter Gruffydd (1935-) was born in Liverpool and spent his youth in Gwynedd. He was educated at the University of North Wales and became a teacher in Llanberis and Rhyl. He is known primarily as a poet and came to prominence in the nineteen-sixties along with such names as Sally Roberts Jones, Herbert Williams and John Idris Jones.

Phil Carradice (1947-) was born in Pembroke Dock. He has published over twenty books, including *The Last Invasion*. He is also active as a short story writer, a broadcaster and researcher and a creative writing tutor. As though all this were not enough, he also finds time to edit *The South Wales Golfer*.

John Sam Jones (1957-) was born in Barmouth and works as a social worker in Denbighshire. He contributes regularly to Welsh language radio and television programmes and has published two English language short story collections. His work focuses to a great extent on gay men.

Angharad Price (1971-) was born in Bangor and read modern languages at Jesus College, Oxford. She was the winner of the Prose Medal at the National Eisteddfod at St David's in 2002 and combines her life as a writer with her post as a lecturer in the Department of Welsh at the University of Cardiff. She has translated much Welsh language poetry into other European languages.

Tristan Hughes (1976-) was born in Canada where he lived for two years before moving to Wales. He was educated at Ysgol David Hughes, Menai Bridge, the Universities of York and Edinburgh and King's College, Cambridge. He now lives on Anglesey and has published The Tower, a volume of short stories which are all set on the island, 'Of Rocks and Men' being one of these.

Acknowledgements

Dafydd Jenkins' translation of Kate Roberts, A Summer Day appeared in *'Welsh Short Stories'*, Faber and Faber; 1959.

J. Walter Jones' translation of 'Dripping Leaves' by W.J. Gruffydd appeared in *'Welsh Short Stories'* edited by Gwyn Jones, published by Penguin; 1940.

Islwyn Ffowc Ellis' translation of John Gwilym Jones' 'The Wedding' was first published in *'Twenty Five Welsh Short Stories'* edited by Gwyn Jones and Islwyn Ffowc Elis and published by the Oxford University Press; 1971. It appears here with the permission of the Estate of the author.

Hywel Teifi Edwards' translation of Alun T. Lewis' 'Relatives' was included in *'The Second Penguin Book of Welsh Short Stories'* edited by Alun Richards (1993).

Eigra Lewis Roberts' 'Deprivation', in Enid R. Morgan's translation appeared in *'Twenty Five Welsh Short Stories'* edited by Gwyn Jones and Islwyn Ffowc Elis. It appears by kind permission of the author.

Emyr Humphreys 'The Arrest' was previously anthologised in John Davies' short story anthology *'The Green Bridge'* (Seren) and, more recently in Dr Humphreys' collection of short stories *'Old People are a Problem'* (Seren; 2003). He has granted his permission for its republication here.

Peter Gruffydd's 'The Circles' first appeared in *'The Works'*, published by the Welsh Union of Writers (1991) and is reproduced with the authors kind consent.

Jane Edwards' 'Now Alone' in the translation by Elin Williams was previously published in *'Planet'* Number 100 (August/September 1993) and is reprinted here by kind permission of the author.

Glenda Beagan's 'Foxy' appeared in *'Magpies'* an anthology edited by Robert Nisbet (Gomer; 2000) and appears here by permission of the author.

We are indebted to Parthian for allowing us to make use of the following stories in these pages:

'The Cuckoos Time is April and May' by Robin Llywelyn, translated by Meic Stephens, appeared in *'The White Afternoon'* edited and translated by Meic Stephens (1998). It originally appeared as 'Amser y Gwcw yw Ebrill a Mai' in *'Y Dur Mawr Llwyd'* (Gomer; 1995)

'The Woman Next Door' by Angharad Price, translated by Meic Stephens' was included in *'The White Afternoon'* edited and translated by Meic Stephens also appears in *'The White Afternoon'*. It originally appeared as 'A Fan Hyn' appeared in *'Straeon Siesta; Rhod y Chwyn'* edited by Delyth George, published by Y Lolfa (1997).

'A House of One's Own' by Siân James appeared in *'Not Singing Exactly'* (Honno 1997) and was subsequently published in *'Outside Paradise'* (2003).

'The Wonder of Seal Cave' by John Sam Jones origianlly appeared in *'Mamma's Baby (Papa's Maybe)'* edited by Arthur Smith and Lewis Davies (1999).

'Of Rocks and Stones' by Tristan Hughes is from *'The Tower'* (2003)

'Like a Duck to Water' by Phil Carradice appears by permission of the author and originally appeared in *'Social Work Today'*. Ours thanks to the author for allowing us to reprint it here.

'The Return' by Brenda Chamberlain appears by kind permission of the Estate of the author.